Thyme to Live

A We Sisters Three Mystery

USA Today Bestselling Author
Melissa F. Miller

Brown Street Books

This book is a work of fiction. Names, characters, places, and incidents either are the product of the author's imagination or are used fictitiously.

Any resemblance to actual persons, living or dead, is entirely coincidental.

This one's for my own sister, whose personality includes a bit of Rosemary, a dash of Sage, and a hint of Thyme.

Acknowledgments

As always, I'm beyond grateful to my crack editing team for polishing my work and to my family for keeping the noise down to a dull roar while I'm writing.

One

"Thigh-me. Thigh-me?"

The barista's flat New York accent cut through my daydream and I squinted at the coffee bar to see if my almond milk chai latte was up. It was.

I jostled my way through the sea of people and snagged the cup.

"You Thigh-me?" the harried woman behind the counter asked. "That's an unusual name."

"It's Thyme, actually," I said for probably the seven thousandth time in my twenty-two years.

"Time for what?" She asked, genuine confusion flooding her face.

"Nothing. Never mind."

I grabbed the steaming cup and elbowed my way out of the crowded shop onto the equally packed sidewalk, silently cursing my parents.

Who names a kid Thyme, anyway? Mary Jane Holloway and Bartholomew Field, that's who. My parents had their children very late in life. Dad was nearing fifty and Mom was well into her forties when my oldest sister, Rosemary, was born. Sage followed eighteen months later. And I brought up the rear fifteen months after that.

In what I have to imagine was a sleep-deprived haze, my parents decided to be good, aging hippies and name their daughters after the old Simon and Garfunkel song "Scarborough Fair."

Oh, I can hear what you're thinking. Don't those lyrics actually go "parsley, sage, rosemary, and thyme"? Yes, yes, they do. But as Mary Jane and Bart would be quick to point out, Parsley is hardly an appropriate name for a child. (They gave it to the cat.)

Thyme, however, is a perfectly reasonable name for your third daughter and should in no way be viewed as a reflection of the fact that your change-of-life birth control method failed.

My name was hardly at the top of the grievance list as far as MJ and Bart were concerned, though. They had done far worse by their daughters than bestowing ridiculous flower power names on us. They had somehow so badly mismanaged the family business—an upscale holistic retreat—that when they stunned us by suddenly gifting us three equal shares of Tranquility by the Sea, the real surprise had been the mountain of debt and half a million dollar balloon payment due twenty-four months out.

Our parents handed over the keys and then sailed off in their houseboat bound for tropical sands out of reach of their personal creditors. Rosemary and Sage had both abandoned their callings to take higher-paying jobs. I'd had one semester left at college, and my sisters had strong-armed me into finishing.

After graduation, instead of enrolling in the psychology Ph.D. program, I'd taken the highest paying job I could find, despite the fact that "personal yogalates instructor to demanding CEO" didn't exactly put my undergraduate degree to good use. Well, I did occasionally have to employ my understanding of reverse psychology on Cate Whittier-Clay to get her to stretch. But, otherwise, no.

Thinking about my client got my heart racing and I reflexively checked my watch. Ten minutes to six. And four long blocks to go. I broke into a jog, keeping a careful grip on the hot drink.

If I was late, she'd blow a gasket. It was critically important that we finish her thirty-minute morning stretch and tone by six thirty and not a moment later.

Her days were scheduled with military precision. Cardio with Rubio from five-thirty to six; then our session; shower, dress, and gulp down a green smoothie from six thirty to six forty-five; spend the next ten to fifteen minutes giving the day's marching orders to her

husband, Evan, and Helena, little Audra's nanny. Finally, she slipped into the back seat of her waiting car
at seven o'clock on the dot for the short drive to her
Wall Street office, where she did whatever it was she
did that enabled her to spend in the mid-six figures
annually on her personal staff—not that I was knock-
ing it, mind you.

I was more than happy to help the Mistress of the
Universe with her pursuit of increased flexibility for
the low, low rate of one hundred and fifty dollars an
hour. Her goal was to execute a perfect center split.
Mine was to have several hundred thousand dollars to
add to the Save the Resort fund by the end of the year.
Thanks to my roster of rich, tense Manhattanites in
search of toning and relaxation, I was well on my way.

Cate was my highest-paying client, though, so I really couldn't set her off and get myself fired. I checked
my watch again and took a big gulp of the chai, scald-
ing my throat with the hot liquid. Then I reluctantly
pitched it into the nearest trash receptacle and ran flat
out the rest of the way to the Whittier-Clay co-op,
skidding through the entrance, which the doorman
managed to jerk open just in time to prevent me from
bouncing off the glass like a confused bird.

"Thanks, Hercules!" I shouted as I raced over to the
elevator bank and pounded the button for the penthouse car.

"Wait, Thyme, hang on." He trailed me to the elevator lobby.

I turned and saw worry in his brown eyes. I liked Hercules. I wasn't sure if it was based mainly on some stupid name solidarity, but he was kind and friendly, unlike almost everyone else I'd run into in this city.

"Is something wrong?"

He grimaced. "I just wanted to warn you."

"Warn me?"

"Helena didn't show up for work today. Mrs. Whittier-Clay's in ... well, she's in a mood."

As the elevator doors opened, my stomach sank. I could only imagine the abuse Cate had rained down on everyone from her husband to the doorman when it became clear the nanny was going to be a no-show. If it was anything like the time her chef had used 1% cow's milk instead of rice milk in her morning smoothie, today was going to be a nightmare.

"Thanks for the head's up," I said, reluctantly forcing myself to step into the waiting elevator car.

He gave me a sickly smile. "Good luck."

The doors closed on his concerned face and the elevator began its ascent to the 4,000 square feet of luxury the Whittier-Clays called home.

I'm gonna need more than luck, I thought. *I'm going to need a miracle.*

~ ~ ~ ~ ~ ~ ~ ~ ~ ~

No miracles came to pass, however, and while Cate bustled around the vast apartment shouting orders on her way out the door, I found myself building a tower out of magnetic tiles with Audra. My efforts to convince Cate that I wasn't a suitable substitute babysitter had been met by a blank look and an arched eyebrow but no verbal response. I just hoped she squeezed in some time to call and lambaste her nanny service into sending over a new one at some point during her day.

Don't get me wrong. I like kids. I just don't really understand them. How was I going to entertain Audra all morning?

As Audra concentrated on balancing a triangular tile on the roof of the structure we'd constructed, I pulled out my cell phone and called an expert.

Sage answered on the second ring.

"Hey, Thyme."

"Hi. Are you busy?"

"Medium busy. Skylar and Dylan are building a sand castle. I just need to supervise. What's up?"

"Cate's babysitter seems to have quit," I whispered into the phone.

I didn't know if Audra was attached to Helena or not, but I didn't want to be the one to break the news. Besides, it was possible Helena was just really sick or something and hadn't been able to call in. Unlikely, given that she would have known the fury that would spark, but possible.

"That's not a shocker. If Cate's as intense as you say, she probably runs through nannies like tissues."

"Tissues? Heaven forbid. Just use a handkerchief."

We shared a laugh at that. Paper products were verboten in our childhood home. Then I got serious. "But Helena didn't call the service or anything. She just ... didn't show up this morning. So take a guess who's watching Audra?"

"You're kidding."

"Nope. I told Cate no, but it was clear she was leaving no matter what I said. What am I gonna do? Leave a three-year old to her own devices? So that's why I'm calling. What do I do with her?"

"Just play with her."

"We're building blocks right now. What else, though? She's going to get bored, isn't she?"

Sage laughed. "She's not an extraterrestrial, Thyme. She's just a small person. Ask her what she wants to do."

She made it sound so easy. I narrowed my eyes suspiciously and glanced at Audra. She was gingerly adding another magnetic tile to her structure. I understood her caution. Those tiles collapsed into a heap if you breathed too hard. But at least she didn't get upset when they fell. Unlike her mother, Audra seemed to be the human embodiment of placid.

"That's it?"

"That's it. Wait—she's three, right?"

"Yeah, I think. Maybe four."

"She might need help in the bathroom."

Yay.

"Okay. Thanks. I should go."

"Hang on. Have you talked to Rosemary today?"

"No. Why?"

"The bank called with an update."

I steeled myself. "Good news or bad?"

"Good, for once."

I exhaled. "Hit me."

"The loan officer reviewed the papers we put together objecting of the sale of the debt back to that scumbag Herk and agreed not to transfer it."

"Really?" I nearly melted into a puddle of relief. "So the terms don't change?"

"The terms don't change, and we don't have to get in bed with a nasty loan shark."

It had been a tense couple of months. We were chugging along, making great progress on paying off the debt, when out of the blue the bank had decided to sell it back to the low-level criminal who'd put the squeeze on our parents in the first place. It had been Sage's idea to come clean with the bank about Herk's less savory activities, and it seemed to have worked.

"You just made my day."

"I know, right? Oh, hey, I gotta run. Dylan's heading for the water."

She ended the call, and I turned my attention back to Audra. If Sage could take care of two preschoolers basically full-time, I could hang with Audra for a morning. How hard could it possibly be?

Two

*V*ery hard, that's how hard. I felt like a wrung-out dishtowel by lunchtime. The sort of noodly, limp feeling that followed an intense hot yoga class. Only instead of working my body to its limits, I'd stretched my imagination to its breaking point.

Audra was a sweet kid. But she was all go, go, go, and no rest. At no point did she just want to veg in front of some educational programming on PBS Kids.

After she tired of the building tiles, we fed and bathed her endless collection of baby dolls, read an assortment of cardboard-backed picture books (some of them a half-dozen times), cooked in her pretend kitchen, and were acting out an elaborate family drama with three stuffed tigers when Hercules called the apartment to let me know a visitor was on the way up.

Hallelujah, the nanny service sent a replacement! I could go home and veg out in front of some grown up educational programming on PBS. Maybe Helena had just needed a mental health day. This nannying stuff was exhausting. I was suddenly grateful that I didn't have any afternoon clients on Mondays.

I handed Audra the mommy tiger, told her I'd be right back, then set off for the door at a near-jog. I yanked it open just as my savior rang the doorbell.

"Hi, you must be from the service," I said, trying to keep my enthusiasm within the bounds of social acceptability.

A baffled man stared at me. He was tall, at least six feet, with an olive complexion and lively brown eyes. He flashed me a tentative smile, and I was blinded by the whitest teeth I'd ever seen other than on a movie screen.

"Uh, sorry, no."

Gah.

"No, I'm sorry. I was expecting a replacement sitter. Audra's nanny didn't show up for work today," I said in an effort to explain my weird, overeager behavior.

The stranger's face dropped and his skin paled to an ashy gray-white. His eyes were wide and full of terror.

"Are you okay?"

"Pardon me," he said, struggling to pull himself together. "I'm looking for Helena. I hoped she'd be here."

Ooooh. Awkward.

"The Whittier-Clays haven't heard from her," I told him gently.

He gripped the doorway and took great gulping breaths as if he were trying to swallow the oxygen.

I didn't know who this guy was—a jilted lover, a landlord looking for the rent, but he sure was taking Helena's absence to heart. I scanned the hallway.

"Why don't you take a seat on that bench over there and I'll bring you a glass of water?"

He nodded and collapsed onto the padded bench with the scrollwork back that was positioned under a gigantic gilt-framed mirror just across the hall from the Whittier-Clays' front door. I watched him for a moment to make sure he wasn't going to pass out or barf on the Persian carpet or anything. He closed his eyes and leaned his head back against the wall.

I shut the door gently and trotted toward the kitchen to get the water. As I passed Audra's playroom I realized that while I definitely couldn't invite a complete stranger into the apartment, I also couldn't leave her alone inside while I talked to him in the hallway. This whole being responsible for a small child thing was fraught with difficulty.

I stopped in the doorway to her room after I fetched the water. The baby tiger was climbing on the daddy tiger's back for some reason.

"Hey, Audra?"

She glanced up at me with somber blue-gray eyes. "Yes?"

"There's a man out in the hall looking for Helena, and he's not feeling very well. Want to come with me to give him some water?"

"Sure," she chirped, dropping the tigers to the carpeted floor. She skipped across the room and slipped her small, warm hand into mine. "Maybe he needs some crackers, too. Helena says crackers will settle your tummy."

"Good idea. We'll ask him."

I returned to the hallway with Audra in tow to find my mystery man holding his head in his hands. His elbows were braced on his knees and he stared down at the plush carpet.

"Hi, mister," Audra said in her little-girl squeak of a voice.

He lifted his eyes at the sound of her voice. It was obvious he'd been crying. His eyes glistened.

"Hi, there. You must be Audra. Helena told me all about you," he said in a hoarse, cracking voice.

"She did?" Audra breathed.

"She sure did. She said you love going to the zoo. The tigers are your favorite."

Audra clapped her hands together in delight. I handed him the glass of water. He took it gratefully and gulped the entire glass in three big swallows.

"Thank you," he said. "I was just so sure I'd find her here."

I cut my eyes toward Audra then said. "How do you know Helena?"

His eyes widened and he shook his head. "Where are my manners? I apologize." He stood and extended a hand. "I'm Victor Callais, Helena's brother."

I smiled. "Thyme Field. I work with Audra's mom. I'm her trainer."

"Ah, yes, the yoga-Pilates woman." He smiled, and his eyes crinkled. That's my favorite—when a guy's eyes smile along with his mouth.

"So you don't know where Helena is either?" I asked, keeping my voice light for Audra's sake.

"No. We were supposed to have brunch yesterday, but she never turned up. She hasn't returned any of my calls, and I had to be up here for a story this morning, so I thought I'd drop by her work and make sure she's okay. I guess she's not." The haunted look returned to his eyes.

"Are you a librarian?" Audra piped up.

We stared down at her in mutual confusion, until finally comprehension dawned on me. "You said you were on the Upper East Side for a story," I explained.

Victor laughed. "No, I'm not a librarian. I'm a reporter. I write stories about things that are happening."

"Magazines? Like my mom."

Victor lifted an eyebrow at the comparison. "Sort of. I work for a newspaper." He glanced at me. "I'm a reporter for the *Times*."

Sure, stringer for *The New York Times* and publishing mogul overseeing a behemoth multimedia empire were totally the same, but the answer suited Audra.

"Maybe you could make a poster for Helena," she suggested. "Like when Mrs. Andreau lost her kitty. She put up a picture of Fluffles in all the elevators. He was in the storage basement chasing mice, and he came home."

He nodded gravely, soaking in her preschool wisdom. "Great idea. Hey, did Helena say anything to you on Friday about taking a trip or going away?" he probed gently.

It struck me that at no time during the morning's crisis had anyone else thought to ask Audra if she knew where Helena might be. One point for the journalist.

Audra thought for a moment then gave her head a shake, sending her long blond ponytail of hair whipping across her shoulders. "No, no trips. But she was crying right before it was time to go home."

"She was crying?" I echoed.

"Uh-huh. I asked her if she hurt herself. She said no, she was crying because she was going to miss me. But then we sang the days of the week song, and I said only two days and then we'd be able to play again.

There's Sunday and there's Monday, there's Tuesday and there's Wednesday, there's Thursday and there's Friday. And then there's Saturday! Days of the week! Bum, bum. Days of the week!"

I giggled at her performance, but Victor blanched again. He swallowed hard. "Thank you, ladies. I've taken up enough of your time." He bent and shook Audra's hand then stood and pulled out a business card.

"Please, if you hear from Helena, call me. That's my cell phone number, day or night." He pressed the card into my hand.

I glanced at it then slipped it into my sweater pocket. "I will," I promised.

Three

I put Helena and her distraught, hot brother out of my mind for the rest of the day. At three o'clock, Cate's assistant called to let me know that Audra's music and movement teacher was on her way over to relieve me.

"Cate wanted me to tell you she's interviewing replacement candidates this evening, and with any luck your services won't be needed tomorrow," she said in a clipped, efficient voice.

I looked sidelong at Audra, who was absorbed in her sticker book.

"Listen, Maura," I said in a near-whisper. "Audra's a great kid, but I have other clients. I'm not canceling appointments to play babysitter. You need to make sure Cate understands that my services aren't an option tomorrow."

I heard Maura's soft sigh through the phone. "Thyme, I can't perform miracles. Believe me. If I could, I would completely squander that talent on keeping Cate's life bump-free. She doesn't care about your other clients. She did say to tell you she'll pay your regular rate for today."

She was paying me a hundred and fifty dollars an hour to watch her kid? It must be nice to solve your problems by reaching into your Birkin bag, grabbing your Valentino wallet, and casually tossing it in the general direction of whatever's troubling you. And, *voila*, problem solved.

"All the same. One of these replacements better work out."

"Agreed. Or, even better, Helena could make an appearance."

That stunned me. "Cate would let her come back?"

Maura laughed. "I know, right? If you or I pulled a stunt like this, it would be *sayonara*, don't let the door hit ya'. But Audra *loves* Helena. And Cate, despite all appearances, dotes on Audra. She'd take Helena back in a heartbeat."

"And the nanny service hasn't heard from her?"

"Nope. And the case manager there said it's virtually impossible that Helena could get another nannying gig in this city without impeccable references, which she obviously won't have."

I thought. "Maybe she's just taking a break, you know? She's socked away some money and plans to bum around." Helena was probably no older than me. Lots of people flake out on their first real jobs.

"Not a chance. She's here on a work visa. If she's not employed, she's gotta go back to Brazil."

"Huh."

"Yeah, huh."

After I ended the call with Maura, I told Audra that Miss Emily was on her way, and she started dancing around her bedroom, clapping her hands.

"I had fun with you today," I told her as I shoved toys into linen bins and generally tried to restore some semblance of order to the place.

"Me, too," she agreed. "Mom says you can leave them. Becky will clean them up when she comes."

I crouched beside her. "Your mom's confused. Even when we're lucky enough to have people to help us keep our houses clean and take care of us, we still need to take care of our own things. Becky's a helper, but you need to be a helper, too."

She wrinkled her little forehead in confusion but, after a moment, joined me in tossing dolls and puzzle pieces into their designated spaces. A moment later, the doorbell rang, and we raced to the door to greet Miss Emily. I didn't know if my subversive act would stick, but for now, I was feeling pretty good about trying to steer Audra off the path of the obliviously wealthy and onto a more thoughtful course. Cate could thank me later—or not, as the case may be.

~ ~ ~ ~ ~ ~ ~ ~ ~ ~

I needed to de-stress, so I popped in for a quick Bikram session at the studio around the corner from the Whittier-Clay's co-op. There's nothing like a one-hundred-and-five-degree yoga class to leave a soul relaxed and placid.

My calm and tranquility were short-lived, though, because when I left the yoga studio I ran into Victor Callais. And when I say 'ran,' I mean I bounced off his well-muscled chest. I was still in my post-yoga noodle state, so he had to reach out and steady me.

"Sorry," I mumbled, acutely aware of the fact that I was slick with sweat. Yes, the studio had a shower, but I prefer a nice long soak in a tub full of lavender essential oils and Epsom salts after a vigorous class. Sue me.

"Thyme, hey!" He seemed inordinately excited to see me.

"Hi." I smiled at him and ever-so-casually raised my arm to take a quick sniff. Eh, passable. Then I noticed the fistful of flyers in his hands and forgot all about my post-workout aroma. He'd taken Audra's advice and made missing person posters. A black-and-white Helena smiled up at me under an all-caps heading that read "Have You Seen Me?"

I nodded at the papers. "She still hasn't turned up?"

He shook his head. His eyes were sad. "No. I posted on all my social media accounts, and as many of hers as I could crack the passwords for—but finally I decided to go old school."

Way across town, my bathtub was calling my name. I could almost hear its siren song from here. But then I imagined about how I'd feel if Rosemary or Sage were missing, and my heart started to hammer in my chest just at the thought. I looked into his bottomless dark brown eyes and sighed. "Let me help you."

Thirty-four telephone poles and coffee shop bill-boards later, we were out of flyers. We stood awkwardly at the corner, avoiding the hot garbage air that rose from the sidewalk grate.

"Well, thanks," he said.

For a journalist, he wasn't very wordy.

"No problem. I hope she's all right." My platitude sounded weak to my own ears, but then again, I wasn't paid by the word.

We nodded at each other, and I shoved my hands into my pockets and turned to leave.

"Wait."

I twisted and looked at him over my shoulder. "Yeah?"

He inhaled deeply and then let out a big, trembly breath. "I'm going to try her apartment one last time. I already hung flyers around her neighborhood. But ... I really don't want to go back to her building by myself. Keep me company?"

His chocolate eyes were pleading. They reminded me of Parsley, my family's cat, when he really wanted someone to sneak him a shrimp or a piece of turkey.

I felt myself giving in. "Where's her place?" If he said Brooklyn or Washington Heights, he was on his own.

"Midtown," he said perkily, almost like he could read my mind.

I shrugged. "Sure. That's on my way."

His shoulders sagged with relief. "I really appreciate this, Thyme."

"I can't imagine how crazy I'd be going if one of my sisters were missing," I told him.

"How many sisters do you have?"

"Two," I answered before I realized he wasn't beside me any longer. I turned and saw him hailing a cab. I'd instinctively headed for the subway station. I joined him at the cab stand in front of some boutiquey hotel I'd never noticed before. "Taxis? Are you independently wealthy?"

He flashed me a smile. "I got my hack license when I first came to your country. Worked my way through Columbia's journalism school driving a cab. Guess I have a soft spot for these guys, you know?"

A cab pulled to a stop alongside us, and Victor opened the door and ushered me into the back seat. He settled in beside me and gave the driver an address—presumably, Helena's—then glanced over at me. "So tell me about your sisters."

"Well, I'm the youngest. Rosemary, the oldest, got her degree in science, but now she runs her own holistic catering company in California. She's dating a homicide detective. Sage is in the middle. She used to be an accountant, but now she's a parenting consultant—basically, a fancy nanny—for a professional golfer and his family in South Carolina. *She's* dating a caddy."

"And you? What did you used to be before you were a personal trainer?"

"I got my psychology degree. I was planning to go to grad school but ..." I trailed off, unsure how to explain my family's financial situation in a pithy way.

"Interesting that you all reinvented yourselves," he mused, more to himself than to me. "And who are *you* dating?"

I blushed. I knew he was just asking because I'd included Sage and Rosemary's relationship statuses in my little summary. But, there was the teensiest chance he was asking because he was interested. And I was currently on boyfriend hiatus after a disastrous breakup with my college sweetheart.

He was watching my face, half-smiling.

I didn't respond. Instead, I turned my face and looked out the window to make it crystal clear that the topic wasn't one I cared to elaborate on. We rode in silence, except for the driver's persistent stream of soft curse words aimed at every New Yorker who dared to cross his path. At least he was quiet about it. Nothing stressed me out more than a cab driver who screamed, red-faced, while pounding his fist on the steering wheel. It sounds like a caricature, I know, but cross-town traffic could bring out the maniacal side of just about anyone. I'd yet to drive in the city, and I hoped to keep it that way.

The cab lurched to a stop in front of a pre-war apartment building. Victor paid the fare and ex-changed some cabbie pleasantries with the driver while I scooted out of the back seat and inhaled the crisp, fall air. As much as I didn't want to drive in New York, riding around as a passenger tended to leave me slight-ly carsick and queasy. I took another deep breath.

"Are you okay?" Victor asked as he joined me on the sidewalk.

I nodded and sneaked a peek at his face. He looked a bit green, himself. Either he was also carsick ... or he was worried about what we might find in his sister's apartment.

My pulse ticked up a notch. I hadn't really consid-ered all the possible ramifications of Helena's disap-pearance, which, in retrospect, was kind of silly of me. I mean, in the past six months, each of my sisters had been involved in a murder investigation. What if death really did come in threes?

Stop that, you sound like Mom with the old wives'
tales. Death doesn't come in threes, fours, or twelve-
packs. It's random, I reassured myself; only, somehow,
that wasn't very reassuring.

I took another look at Victor and swallowed around
the lump in my throat. "Do you have a key to Helena's
place?"

He shook his head. "No."

I waited but apparently he was going to leave his
answer at a terse, one-worder.

"So then, what's your plan?" I pressed him as we
walked up the wide stairs to the row of buzzers beside
the double front doors to the building. This wasn't a
doorman building, that much was clear.

"It's a work in progress," he muttered cryptically,
scanning the rows of typewritten names, some yellowed
with age, some curling up at the edges, and others
brand-spanking new.

I peered over his shoulder. He pressed the button
beside "V. Smith."

"Who's that?"

"That's Helena's apartment."

"V. Smith?"

He gave me a sidelong glance. "It's urban safety
101, Thyme. Please tell me your buzzer label doesn't
identify you as a single woman living alone?"

One, I highly doubted that 'Thyme' screamed 'I'm a
lady.' But, two, just in case, I did list my name as "T.

Field" everywhere because I wasn't actually an idiot. I didn't use a pseudonym, though.

"No, it doesn't," I assured him. "But why 'Smith'? Isn't her last name Callais, like yours?" I asked knowing full well that it was.

He either didn't hear the question or pretended not to. He laid on the buzzer again. After a moment, he sighed. "No answer."

I squinted at the buzzer labels. "Do you know which of these is the building super?"

"I do, but he's a dead end. I called him this morning and he said the only way he's letting me into Helena's apartment is if I have the boys in blue with me."

I shrugged. I could kind of see the guy's point. Helena was an adult. If she just happened to have met her dream man over the weekend, and they were holed up in her bedroom with a vat of whip cream or a family-sized bottle of baby oil, it would be pretty awful to come storming in with her brother.

"Have you considered calling them? The police, I mean?"

"No. Not yet." His face darkened.

I decided not to push the issue. "Okay? So are we going to hang out here until someone comes home and try to talk our way in, or what?" I shifted my weight from one foot to the other. I mean, it wasn't *cold*, but it wasn't warm. And as the autumn sun dropped lower and lower in the sky, it was only going to get cooler.

Already, my dried hot yoga sweat was giving me a slight chill—at least I hoped that was the cause of my shivering.

He flashed me a smile. "Watch and learn."

He started at the uppermost button on the far left. He gave it one short press, waited a moment to see if there would be a response, and then moved to the button to its immediate right. It was late afternoon on a weekday, so assuming most of the apartment dwellers in Helena's building worked, the majority of them were unlikely to be home. He kept pressing, moving left-to-right, top-to-bottom, in search of a shift worker, a stay-at-home parent, or a retiree. On the eleventh button, he got a hit.

"Who is it?" a distorted male voice answered.

I checked the label. 'Bizwan Malta.' Works from home in tech support, I guessed, based on nothing.

"This is Victor Callais. I'm a reporter with *The New York Times*. I'm doing a man on the street feature about the mayor's latest crime-prevention initiative and wondered if you'd like to share your thoughts?"

"I'm not on the street. And no." Bizwan dismissed him and went back to helping a frustrated computer user reinstall Windows 8.1 or whatever it was he'd been doing before his buzzer had interrupted him.

Undeterred, Victor resumed his relentless march through the buzzers.

He had another hit on the nineteenth try.

"Yes?" A cautious female voice answered. Apparently, its owner had taken urban safety 101. The nameplate read 'Keith Binder.'

"Hi, my name's Victor Callais. I'm a reporter with *The New York Times*, and I wanted to ask Mr. Binder his views on the new magnet school that's being proposed for this neighborhood."

"Oh. Um, he's ... not here right now. But I—we—don't have kids, so I don't think we have an opinion. You should try Mrs. Chandra in 4-B."

He hovered his finger over the button marked 'Chandra.' "She's a parent of school-aged children?" he asked.

"No, but she's a retired teacher. And a talker." 'Keith' gave a short laugh, as though Mrs. Chandra had waylaid her more than once with an armload of groceries for a nice long chat.

"Perfect. Thanks so much!"

"No problem."

He grinned at me and then pressed Mrs. Chandra's buzzer. As promised, she was more than willing to share her thoughts about the state of public education. After about a minute and a half, she paused to take a breath, and Victor pounced.

"Would you mind if I come inside? The intercom system makes it hard to hear you, and I want to be sure to quote you accurately. Perhaps we can talk in the hallway?" he suggested.

There were several seconds of silence. I imagined Mrs. Chandra was weighing her safety against her loneliness and desire for the limelight. "I suppose that would be all right. I'm on the fourth floor. I'll meet you in the hallway." A long metallic click sounded, and Victor pushed open the door.

We were in.

"Now what?" I whispered as he hurried passed the rows of metal mailboxes and through an interior door.

"Now we take the stairs to the second floor," he said, pushing open a metal fire door and ushering me into a dimly lit stairwell.

"What about Mrs. Chandra?"

He shrugged. "She'll get tired of waiting and go back inside. She'll forget all about us in no time."

I tried to shake the icky feeling that I got thinking of the gregarious old lady waiting a few floors above and mounted the stairs behind him.

Four

e came to a stop outside Helena's door. He rattled the knob. I shifted nervously and checked the hallway for traffic. There was none. No residents headed to the laundry room. In fact, it was eerily quiet. No televisions blared from behind the rows of closed doors. No voices raised in conversation or argument floated out into the hallway. The only sounds I heard were my own shallow breathing and my thrumming heartbeat.

The only evidence that the second floor was inhabited at all was the faint aroma of stale curry that hung in the air like a cloud. As an apartment dweller myself, I'd recognize that smell anywhere. The mayor's next initiative should be to require all Indian takeout to be eaten with a window open. Or to install functioning exhaust fans in the city's apartment buildings. Something.

I shook my head and pulled myself back to attention. Presumably, we were about to break into Helena's apartment. I supposed I should be paying closer attention, so that I could at least testify against Victor and get myself a better deal when we got convicted. I wondered idly if Rosemary's boyfriend would write me a character reference, and, if so, how much weight the word of a Los Angeles detective would carry with New York law enforcement.

And then, Victor gave the doorknob another turn. It swung open.

He turned and looked at me, wide-eyed and pale-faced. Apparently, he was as surprised as I was to find it unlocked.

"Now what?"

In answer, he gulped and stepped across the threshold.

Please don't let her be having a baby oil party. I sent out my plea to the universe and followed him inside.

He reached behind me and pulled the door shut gently.

Or dead, I quickly amended. *Please don't let us find Helena's decomposing body. Especially not dead in the middle of a baby oil party.*

We stood just inside the doorway and surveyed the small apartment. The galley kitchen was dark. From what I could see, no glasses or dishes sat in the sink.

But that didn't mean much. The average kitchen in a New York apartment was too old and dated to support much cooking. Its highest and best use was as supplemental closet space. Myself, I stored my sweaters in my oven and used my pantry as a shoe rack.

My gaze traveled over the living space. A tired-looking lumpy sofa and a pale blond IKEA coffee table faced a computer monitor that probably doubled as Helena's television. A print from the Museum of Modern Art hung over the couch. Some magazines and junk mail spilled off the coffee table in a pile.

"Helena?" Victor called. His voice wobbled and cracked.

We listened for a moment. No answer.

"'Lena?" he repeated in a louder, stronger voice.

Silence.

He glanced at me and inclined his head toward the short hallway that no doubt led to the bathroom and bedroom. I tried to swallow but my throat was suddenly paper-dry. I nodded.

He reached for my hand as we inched forward. I was surprised by the gesture, but I welcomed it. I was about ready to jump out of my skin, and his warm, strong hand gripping mine provided instant security.

We reached the tiny bathroom. The door was open, and we stepped inside. It was standard-issue. White subway tile on the floor and walls. A cracked porcelain sink with nowhere for a girl to place her toiletries. Helena, or some previous occupant of the apartment, had combatted the lack of counter space by hanging a small glass shelf under the mirrored medicine cabinet. A toothbrush holder with one lone toothbrush, a hairbrush, and a half-empty tube of toothpaste sat on the shelf. If Helena was anything like me, the narrow medicine cabinet would be filled to capacity with creams, lotions, pills, and potions, jammed inside in a jumble that threatened to spill out every time the door swung open.

I surveyed the rest of the room. Toilet jammed up against the outside wall. Short tub, too small for a soak, with a shower head sticking out of the tile above. Helena's shampoo, conditioner, body wash, and razor were lined up on the edge of the tub like soldiers waiting for their orders. I peered down at the bottom of the tub. No water droplets gathered near the drain.

I reached out and touched the fluffy pink towel that hung from the bathroom's only hook. Also dry.

Victor watched me, and then he stretched his arm forward and touched the bristles on her toothbrush.

"Dry," he said.

My heart ramped up even faster. I wondered just how fast it could go before it exploded in my chest.

"Maybe she went away for the weekend," I suggested.

"Without her toothbrush?"

I didn't have an answer for that, so I said nothing. I flipped open a white wicker hamper that sat in the corner beside the sink and looked inside. My racing heart stopped for a moment, and I froze.

"Victor," I said when I finally found my voice. "You should see this."

He gave me a curious look and leaned forward. I knew the exact moment he spotted the blood-soaked pink towel because he inhaled sharply. He reached for the towel, and I placed a hand on his arm to stop him.

"You shouldn't touch it. Fingerprints," I explained haltingly.

He nodded. Then he just stood there, staring down into the hamper.

I gave his sleeve a gentle tug. "We need to get out of here and call the police."

He didn't move for a moment. Then he dragged his eyes up to mine. "Let's take a quick look at her bedroom."

Noooooo. Oh, hell, no, my mind was screaming at me to get out of this apartment pronto. But I imagined finding a bloody towel one of my sisters' bathrooms and just walking out, and I couldn't. I knew I wouldn't.

I gulped. "Okay, but make it *really* quick."

He gave me a 'don't worry about it' look. "Trust me. I don't want to hang around in here any longer than we have to."

He led the way, and I forced myself to put one foot in front of the other and follow him down the short hallway to the bedroom. The door was slightly ajar but not open wide enough that we could actually see inside the room. There could be anything on the other side of the door. Helena's bloody corpse. Or an armed, maniacal serial killer. Or ... he pushed the door all the way open with his foot ...

Nothing.

I let out a breath that I didn't realized I'd been holding. There was nobody (and, more importantly, no body) inside. Just Helena's empty bed and a bedside table against one wall and a shabby-chic dresser with its top drawer pulled out along the other. The dresser was pushed up against the wall near the window. One side of the curtain was stuck between the wall and the dresser. I crossed the room and peered out the window. A fire escape landing sat just below the window. I looked down. The rusted, metal fire escape dropped off into a narrow, filthy alley.

I back turned to Victor, but his attention was fixed on a small, velvet jewelry box that sat on the bedside table. It was empty.

"Something wrong?"

He jumped, startled at the sound of my voice, and flicked his eyes up to meet mine. "What? No. I just ..." He trailed off and stuffed the box into his inside jacket pocket without further comment or explanation. Then he shifted his attention to the bed behind me. "I take that back. Something is wrong."

I followed his gaze. The bed looked pretty normal to me. A queen-sized mattress sat on a cheap wood frame. Green and purple striped sheets that I recognized as being from the Target Home Collection were more or less smoothed over the lumpy mattress. Two standard pillows and a matching decorative sham completed the ensemble.

"What's the matter?"

"Where's her comforter? She has the coordinating comforter."

"Purple and green polka dots?"

He wrinkled his forehead. "As a matter of fact, yes. How did you—?"

"Fellow Target shopper," I told him. "It's pretty lightweight. I use mine year-round."

"So does Helena."

We both stared down at the bed. I'm not sure what was going through his mind, but speaking for myself, I was regretting the steady diet of Lifetime movies I'd binged on the year I moved out of my parents' screen-free home. It was a sure bet, in a made-for-TV movie, at least, that Helena's dead body was currently wrapped up in her lightweight but warm comforter. Probably jammed in one of the Dumpsters that lined the alley below.

As it turns out, his imagination wasn't quite as quick to take a turn for the morbid.

"Maybe she sent it out to be dry cleaned," he mused.

I bit down on my tongue to stop myself from informing him that part of the beauty of that particular bargain comforter was that it was machine washable. But he was waiting for me to validate his fantasy, so I mumbled, "Maybe."

I started to walk toward the door hoping he'd take the hint and follow me out, but instead he pulled open the bifold doors to the bedroom closet.

I squeezed my eyes shut. *No dead bodies, please.* Then I sort of peeked between my eyelids to see if my quick request of the universe had worked.

It had. Sort of.

There were no dead bodies in Helena's closet. What there was, though, was one green and purple polka-dotted comforter drenched in blood.

~ ~ ~ ~ ~ ~ ~ ~ ~ ~

I dragged Victor away from his sister's apartment and down the stairs. I burst through the building's front doors and stood on the cement stoop, sucking down the polluted air in huge gulping breaths as if it were the freshest post-storm sea breeze imaginable.

Beside me, Victor sagged against the wall, gray-faced and silent.

"I'll go with you," I said softly.

He turned and gave me a searching look. "Where am I going?"

"To the police station."

We stared at each other for a beat.

"Aren't you?" I asked.

"No."

"No? Why on earth not? Your sister's missing, and there's blood all over her apartment. No, *worse*, somebody cleaned up the blood that must have been all over her apartment!" I realized I was shouting when a dog walker strolling by with four large dogs shot me a look. I lowered my voice to a near-whisper. "Sorry."

"Look, we need to go somewhere where we can talk." He spoke in a deliberately calm voice, as if he were narrating a guided meditation.

I narrowed my eyes. "We can talk in the back of a cab on the way to the police station."

"Thyme. Please." His dark brown eyes burned into mine, somewhere between pleading and demanding. "I need to explain some things. Let me buy you a cup of coffee. Or a mug of chai? A kale smoothie? Whatever someone like you would drink."

"Scotch," I told him. "One ice cube. I know a place." I raised my arm to hail a cab.

Duke's wasn't fancy. Okay, it wasn't even nice. But it was around the corner from my apartment, and the bartenders there were used to seeing me in workout clothes. Don't get me wrong, I'd visited my share of hip, subterranean whiskey bars, kicked back on couches with a pricy craft single malt, and done the whole girl in the city thing. But, Duke's was home. And not only because Petra, the pink-haired bartender, routinely served me Macallan 18 and charged me for the 12.

My escort didn't seem to share my enthusiasm for the joint, which, in light of the building's peeling facade and poor lighting, was understandable. I dragged him away from the taxi and through the narrow entryway to the bar proper.

Petra waved at me. "The usual?"

"Yeah, but ring it up correctly—he's buying." I jabbed a thumb toward Victor, earning a laugh from Petra.

"You got it. What'll it be for you, big spender?" she asked him.

"Uh ..." he scanned the chalkboard that hung over the bar. "How about a Dark and Stormy?"

"Grab a seat. I'll bring 'em right over."

She hustled to the other end of the mostly empty bar to pour our drinks. I looked around for a table where the handful of patrons wouldn't overhear us.

"Let's sit over there," I suggested, pointing toward a two-top in the front right corner of the bar.

"Sure. Lead the way."

We situated ourselves at the worn wooden table. He propped his elbows against the table's edge and leaned forward. "I guess I owe you an explanation."

"I wouldn't say that," I countered, even though that's *exactly* what I'd say.

I definitely wanted to know what was going on. But at the same time, I wasn't so sure I wanted to get myself in any deeper. During the short cab ride from her apartment to Duke's, it occurred to me that, maybe, the less I knew about Helena's situation, the better. I know that sounds cold, but it's not like she and I were friends, or even acquaintances. We had the same employer, but we rarely, if ever, interacted. She was just another twenty-something woman in a sea of New York women. Except for the fact that she was missing. And all that blood in her apartment.

"You should know," he insisted as Petra walked over with our drinks and a vinyl check holder. She placed the drinks on the table and put the bill near his elbow then gave me a wink. It was standard operating procedure. If I brought a new guy into Duke's, she'd tally up the drinks after the first round. That way, I'd have an easy out if the date turned weird or unpleasant. Petra was probably only in her early thirties, but she acted like a mom sometimes. It didn't bother me at all.

It was nice to have someone looking out for me in a huge, busy city.

I had Petra. And Helena had Victor. I sighed then took a sip of my Scotch and let its pleasant, slow burn make its way down my throat to my belly. "Okay, let's hear it. Why don't you want to go to the police for help?"

He ignored his drink and kept his eyes fixed on mine. "Because the authorities here can't help Helena."

"What does that even mean?"

"It's complicated."

I eyed him over my glass and waited. Finally he said, "Helena moved here from Brazil, just like I did."

"I figured."

"Right, only, unlike me, she didn't move to the states to get her education or for a job opportunity."

"I'll bite. Why did she move here?"

He took a long drink then said, "She was running away."

"From what?" I asked quietly. Something in his face told me I wasn't going to like the story he was about to tell.

"From her husband. When she was seventeen, she married—over our parents' objections—a man named Gabriel. He was much older than Helena, almost a decade. And he had ... a reputation."

"Was he involved in the drug trade?" I knew from listening to the news that Brazil had a high violent crime rate, thanks in large part to drug trafficking and gang warfare.

He shook his head. "Not the way you think. Gabriel was on the Rio police force, but he was—is—corrupt. There's been a pervasive problem with corruption, especially in Rio, and the government has been working to clean it up. But it runs deep, and Gabriel has a lot of friends. As it turned out, he also had a temper. When Helena realized he would eventually kill her, she had nowhere to turn. The authorities would have laughed in her face."

I shuddered. "I can't even imagine."

"It was a bad situation. I was already living in New York, so I helped her run. She's here legally, just so we're clear. I had to ask a lot of people for favors. And I set her up with the nanny service so she'd have work."

"So you think her husband found her?"

He gripped his glass so hard I thought it would shatter in his hands. "I'm afraid he did. He vowed he'd track her down and kill her."

"I'm sorry, but I still don't understand why you don't think the police would help. There's all that blood—"

"I think he found her, yes." He took a shuddering breath. "And I think she's probably dead." Tears shone in his eyes but he blinked them back and downed his drink. "But there's a chance she's just injured, and she's on the run. So I can't go to the police. Gabriel's worked closely with your federal Drug Enforcement Agency on cross-border cases. For all I know he has friends in the NYPD narcotics unit. He's connected. If I enlist law enforcement help in finding her, I'll lead him right to her. I can't risk it."

"You can't do *nothing*, Victor. Your sister—if she's alive—needs help."

"I'm not going to do nothing. I'm going to find her. The question is: will you help me?"

Five

"Nooooooo. No. No. No. Oh, hell, no."

I held the phone away from my ear and waited for my oldest sister Rosemary to calm down. When I heard her pause to take a breath, I jumped in to explain. "You guys, you don't understand. She's his *sister*. What if it were one of you—"

Sage, our middle sister, cut me off mid-sentence. "Let me stop you right there. If one of us ever goes missing, you should go to the cops. The PO-lice." She put heavy emphasis on the first syllable, which made me wonder how much of an accent she was picking up down there in Nowhere, South Carolina.

Focus, Thyme.

"Are you two even listening to me? Victor can't go to the police. She might be running from her psychotic, policeman ex-husband." I was getting exasperated now. These sisterly conference calls usually seemed like a good idea when Rosemary or Sage needed advice. But now it just seemed like a convenient way for them to gang up on me.

"Thyme," Rosemary said in a careful, conciliatory tone, "let's think this through. If the story this guy told you is true, Helena's ex-husband is a very bad dude. That's a reason to go to the authorities, not a reason *not* to."

I exhaled and got ready to explain Rio de Janeiro's culture of corruption for the umpteenth time.

But she wasn't finished. "I know, I heard, he's a dirty cop. And I guess your new friend thinks he has his hooks in dirty cops here, too? Or something? That's ludicrous. It's not like they have international crooked cop conventions. Please don't get mixed up in this. Let me have Dave make some calls."

"What's Dave going to do, Rosie? Los Angeles is all the way on the other side of the country. I don't think he knows every homicide detective in the United States. No offense."

"None taken. But you'd be surprised. The police who aren't busy breaking the law actually *do* get together at conventions, you know. He goes to conferences and stuff. And he may even have had a case where he had to coordinate with the NYPD. It could happen—it's more likely than the notion that this Gabriel guy has a connection there. Will you at least let me talk to him before you go running off to play private investigator with a total stranger?"

I gnawed on my lower lip and thought. It seemed like such a reasonable request. Harmless even. But what if Victor was right? What if Helena's ex-husband did have friends in law enforcement and it got back to him that Dave Drummond, a homicide detective in California, was asking questions? I could be putting Dave—and Rosemary—in danger.

"It's a good idea, Thyme," Sage urged.

I bit down so hard on my lip that I tasted blood. *Ouch.*

"No. I'm sorry, but I don't feel comfortable getting Dave involved. I mean, I appreciate the offer, but I don't want to get him, or you, mixed up in something ugly." I could hear my sisters gathering their breath to continue their lecture, so I hurried on. "Wait. Let me finish. I hear you, okay?" I paused. "And you're right. Of course, you're right. I'll tell Victor I can't help him."

"Really?" Sage pressed, clearly suspicious about my change of heart.

I gave a little laugh. "Really. I mean, I don't know what I was thinking. How could *I* help him anyway?"

"Hey, don't beat yourself up for caring. You've always been so kindhearted," Rosemary said gently.

"That's the truth," Sage agreed. "Bringing home strays, organizing charity drives. I know your instinct is always to help. It's what makes you Thyme. But this just isn't something you can help with."

"Yeah." I waited a beat, then I yawned. "You guys are right, as usual. Thanks for talking me through it. But I'm pretty beat. It's been a stressful day. I think I'm going to turn in early."

"Are you sure you're okay?" Sage asked.

"Positive."

"You take good care," Rosemary said.

"You, too. I love you guys."

They chorused a response and we ended the call.

I folded myself backward into a deep backbend and held the position until I felt the tension drain from my muscles. Then I stood up, grabbed a black hooded sweater from the top shelf of my closet, pulled it on over my black long-sleeve shirt and leggings, and crammed my feet into my running shoes. I rummaged in my nightstand for the small flashlight I kept in case of a power outage. I flipped it on to confirm the batteries still worked then slipped it into my pocket.

I took one last look around the apartment before I let myself out, locked the door behind me, and jogged downstairs to the lobby where Victor was waiting for me.

Six

While I'd been busy arguing with my sisters, Victor had been working the phones, too. By the time I met him in my lobby, he'd arranged to borrow a sedan from a friend who ran a car service. They must have been pretty good friends because the sleek black Lincoln pulled up alongside my building while Victor was still filling me in. A moment later, a second, identical sedan pulled in behind it.

The driver of the first car got out, shook Victor's hand, and pressed the spare keys to the idling car into his palm. After a brief exchange, conducted in Spanish (which meant I was in the dark as to its substance), the driver hopped into the passenger seat of the second car and melted into the cross-town traffic.

Victor yanked the door open for me, and I ducked into the car. It was a perfectly serviceable car, spotlessly clean and fresh-smelling. It had a sort of faded luxury and was easily five or six steps above a public cab in terms of comfort but still a world away from the chauffeured limousine that ferried Cate and her family around. Thinking of the Whittier-Clays brought my mind back to Helena and the purpose of our late-night jaunt.

I buckled my seatbelt and glanced over at Victor, who was intently studying the backlit dashboard.

"So where are we headed?" I asked.

He frowned at the display and held up a finger. "Give me a second."

I watched in silence as he reached into his jacket pocket and removed a small, slim device. It had a black rubberized antenna-looking thing which was connected by a piece of metal to a box with an end that was designed to fit into the cigarette lighter. He plugged it in.

"What is that?"

"A GPS signal jammer."

"Don't you trust your friend to know where we're going?" I squirmed in my seat. The notion of being untraceable made me slightly nervous, as it finally hit me that I didn't actually *know* this guy. *Great time to think it through, Thyme.*

"What? No, no. It's not like that. I trust Jorge with my life. I'm trying to protect him. He's from Rio originally, too. I've known him since we were kids. When I came here, he's the one who got me a job driving cabs.

But, Gabriel also knows him. If he's in the country and he hasn't found Helena, he'll eventually come looking for Jorge. I'd like to give my friend plausible deniability, if nothing else. You see?" He wrinkled his brow in concern.

I considered his answer. "I guess that makes sense," I allowed. "But why do you even have that thing? Is it legal?"

He studied my face and answered slowly. "No, it's not legal. Sometimes, I want to be able to deny having met with a source."

His explanation was plausible, but I could feel myself resisting this whole plan. "I guess I'm getting cold feet," I explained.

He paused and searched my face. "Thyme, if you want to bail out now, I'll understand."

I looked at him for a long moment. Dark blue half-circles were forming under his eyes, highlighting his weekend of worry and fatigue. I thought of the bloodied towel and bedding in Helena's apartment. I swallowed around the lump in my throat. "I'm in. I'd just really like to know where we're going and what the plan is."

He smiled, checked his mirrors, and eased the sedan into the travel lane. "That seems fair. To answer your first question, we're going to visit a friend of Helena's. Lynn was a nanny for a family in the Whittier-Clay's building for a while. Helena used to run into her at the playground, Audra's music class, that sort of thing. They struck up a friendship."

"You said this Lynn used to be a nanny. What's she doing now?"

"She's an actor. She's in a musical running in the East Village. The show ended about twenty minutes ago, so right now she's probably nursing a glass of wine at an Italian restaurant around the corner from the theater waiting for us."

"We're going to dinner?" I looked down at my outfit and shrugged. I guess cat burglars, Johnny Cash, and urbanites all shared an affinity for black. I wouldn't be *too* out of place.

"Lynn likes her pasta. And we need to eat sometime. I don't think Duke's cocktails can fuel us forever."

"Fair enough. Helena's been in touch with Lynn recently?"

He kept his eyes on his mirrors and executed a lane change while he answered. "They got their nails done together on Friday and then did some shopping, according to Lynn. She's the best lead we have right now. As far as I know, she's the last person to have seen Helena."

I settled back into the seat and watched the buildings pass by in a blur of light. Most of my travels around the city were on foot or via the subway. Everything looked different from this perspective. New York

seemed at once busier and smaller. And more dangerous, I hastily added, as a city bus laid on its horn and
muscled its way into the space we were currently occu-
pying. I squeezed my eyes shut as he slid the car into
the parking lane to evade the oncoming bus. There
weren't enough relaxation meditations in the world to
get me behind the wheel of a car in this city. Not on
your life.

I focused on my breathing until we made the turn
onto FDR Drive. Then I felt my shoulders relaxing just
a bit and felt calm enough to converse. "How well do
you know this actress friend?"

"She and Helena are pretty tight. I've met her a few
times at happy hours and stuff." He coughed into his
fist. "And Helena set us up on a few dates."

"You're dating her?" This had the potential to be
awkward. Also, why wasn't his girlfriend helping him?
Especially if she and his sister are friends?

He shook his head. "No. We went out a few times.
She's a great girl, we just didn't hit it off—nothing in
common."

"Oh."

After a moment's silence, he said, "I'm not seeing
anyone right now."

I had no idea how to respond to that. *Me neither? I
didn't ask? Are you on OkCupid?* There didn't seem to
be a good answer, so I just nodded and stared blankly
out the window as we made our way through the unfa-

miliar neighborhoods. I hadn't spent much time exploring the East Village, aside from one weekend when my sisters had visited and we'd zipped through in a whirlwind of appetizers and craft beers.

He cleared his throat a couple of times but, otherwise, we drove in silence until he pulled into a small parking garage sandwiched between a Chinese takeout joint and a rental car office. It was so tight inside that I found myself reflexively ducking as we drove up the ramp.

He eased the Lincoln into a spot and killed the engine. As we headed for the exit, I was glad to see him walking toward the stairwell. This was not the sort of establishment where I'd trust the elevator to work flawlessly—if at all.

I giggled, and he turned to give me a quizzical look. I pointed to the white metal sign affixed to the wall next to the metal door. Red letters warned: *Pedestrian Parking Only.*

"Why would you park a pedestrian?" I laughed,

He frowned at the sign in confusion. "I literally can't even imagine what that sign is trying to convey. What ...?"

He stared at the strange verbiage, transfixed, until I tugged on his sleeve. "Come on. Let's solve one mystery at a time."

~ ~ ~ ~ ~ ~ ~ ~ ~ ~

Lynn was waiting for us at a booth near the back of the packed restaurant. She stood and waved as the host led us through the sea of tables toward her. Lynn looked like an actress. She was tall and thin. Her hair tumbled over her shoulders in a cascade of bouncy copper-colored curls. Her bright green eyes were shadowed, mascaraed, and lined to perfection. Her glossy lipstick matched her hair color. A statement necklace set off her creamy collarbone.

I was suddenly hyper-aware of my post-yoga, head-to-toe black, disheveled appearance. I tried to take a discreet whiff of myself, but thanks to my surroundings all I could smell was garlic, crusty bread, and strong coffee. My stomach rumbled appreciatively.

"Victor!" Lynn called as we approached. She smiled broadly at him and came out from behind the table to sweep him into a hug.

I could feel the host giving me a sympathetic look and unconsciously stood up straighter. Like I always told my clients, posture is everything. I imagined a string connecting the top of my head to the ceiling.

"Lynn, this is Thyme," Victor said as he extricated himself from her embrace and gestured toward me.

She extended a slim hand. "Hi. What an interesting name."

"Thanks." I shook her cool hand and settled myself in the booth across the table from her.

Victor hesitated in the aisle, swiveling his head from Lynn to me and back. She sat down and patted the booth next to her. He eased in beside me, and I felt an unattractive, but undeniable, little thrill of victory.

Lynn didn't show any sign of reacting to his choice. She rested her forearms on the table and gestured to the menus. "I hope you don't mind, but I went ahead and ordered for the table. I'm always famished after a show, but I hate eating in front of people who are waiting for their food. So, I just ordered a bunch of half-portions to share. Oh, and a bottle of Chianti."

It was a perfectly reasonable, even warm, gesture. And yet, it didn't sit right with me. It was presumptuous, or overbearing, or ... something. I sneaked a peek at Victor's face. From the way his jaw was set, I suspected he wasn't thrilled about Lynn's move, either. I was beginning to see why they hadn't made a love match, despite the fact that the woman was flipping gorgeous.

"That's fine," he said flatly.

Just then, two members of the wait staff arrived in a flurry of dishes, goblets, and goodies. After my first bite of spicy rapini tortellini, washed down with a sip of wine, I forgave Lynn for being pushy. After a mouthful of the crusty, yet soft, Italian bread dipped in warm olive oil, I was ready to date her myself. We devoured the food in silence for a few moments.

Then Lynn said, "So, what's going on with Helena?"

Victor had been mopping up some stray marinara on his plate with a hunk of bread. In response to her question, he pushed the plate aside and let out a long breath. "She's missing."

She froze, her wineglass halfway to her lips. "Missing?" After a beat, she took a drink. "What do you mean?"

His voice was grave, urgent, persuasive all at once. "Let's start at the beginning. Friday afternoon, Helena started to cry at work and told Audra she was going to miss her, which, you know, is odd."

She nodded her agreement. I felt myself mirroring the movement.

"Then, on Sunday morning, we were supposed to meet for brunch at that Greek diner she likes near her gym."

"Theo's?"

"Right. She never showed. I called her a couple times, but she didn't answer. This morning, I still hadn't heard from her and she still wasn't picking up her phone, so I stopped by her place. She didn't answer her door buzzer, and the super wouldn't let me in."

"Where does she come in?" Lynn pointed her fork in my direction, but addressed the question to Victor as if I weren't there.

I gave her a look, but my priority was the calamari, not her manners. It wasn't the typical fried, rubbery calamari—you know, the stuff that's best served drowning in marinara sauce. This was perfectly grilled, lemony and garlicky, with a hint of spice. I speared another piece and let Victor field the question. After all, she was his friend or girlfriend or whatever. His problem, not mine. Plus, the more talking they did, the more eating I could do.

"Thyme works with Audra's mother. She was at the penthouse, watching Audra, when I went to see if anyone there knew where Helena was."

She eyeballed me. "You work with Cate Whittier-Clay? Doing what?"

It was hard to be offended. I hardly looked the part of media maven. "I'm her trainer. Every morning, she does some Pilates, yoga, a little bit of barre work. When Helena didn't show up this morning, she more or less roped me into taking care of Audra until she could find a replacement."

That got a little laugh and a nod out of her. "I can see that. Helena says Cate's a piece of work."

Victor brought the conversation back around to the subject at hand. "Anyway, Thyme was kind enough to help me put up some missing person flyers when she got off work. I convinced her to keep helping me."

"I'll bet you did. You can be *verrrry* persuasive." Her tone was thick with innuendo.

He ignored it. "Right. So we went to Helena's place to check one more time. We actually let ourselves in and looked around, but she wasn't there." I noted that he omitted the whole blood everywhere thing. I wondered whether Helena had confided in Lynn about her past.

Lynn popped a cherry tomato into her mouth and chewed. She had a contemplative expression on her face, as if she was deep in thought. "So, no one's heard from her since I saw her on Friday night?"

"Right. Exactly. As far as I know, you were the last person to see her."

Her green eyes clouded a bit. "She seemed okay," she said haltingly in a tone that suggested she didn't believe her own words.

"Just okay?" Victor pressed.

"Yeah, just okay. She wasn't her usual bubbly self, but she didn't say that anything was wrong. She was just kind of quiet. We went for manicures. She didn't really say much when we were in the salon. But when we went to check out, the cashier told me Helena had already paid my bill." She tapped her glittery, red-gold nails against her glass. I had to admit, her manicure looked pretty good. I curled my own unpolished fingernails into my palms.

"Why would she do that?" Victor asked.

She shrugged. "I don't know. It was kind of weird, but she said she just wanted to thank me for being such a good friend to her."

A parting goodbye gift? Right on the heels of her tearful conversation with Audra about missing her, too. Helena was starting to sound like a person who knew, or at least suspected, that her days were numbered.

An involuntary shiver raced down my spine, and I pushed my dish away. I placed my linen napkin over the uneaten food.

Beside me, Victor looked as though he'd lost his appetite, too. He coughed into his fist and cleared his throat. "And after the nail salon, you went shopping, right?"

"Right."

"Clothes shopping?"

"No." She shook her head and gave a half-laugh. "That was kind of strange, too. We usually window shop at the boutiques, maybe find a shoe sale or pick up some accessories—you know, high-end shopping on a low-end budget."

"Sure," I said, nodding. I knew that particular type of shopping spree all too well, as it happened.

"But on Friday, she wanted to shop for really stupid, boring things."

"Like what?" Victor asked.

She looked up at the ceiling and searched her memory. Then she ticked off the items on her fingers. "Like a blender; new sheets; a travel toothbrush. Oh, and fishing line, for some unknown reason. I mean, we spent the whole time in Tar-jey," she said, placing an ironic French accent on Target's name.

Victor had pulled a mini-notebook out of his breast pocket and was scrawling furiously with a stubby little pencil.

"Does your sister fish?" I asked him.

"Not as far as I know." He finished scribbling his notes and turned back to Lynn. "So, after Target, what did you do?"

"Okay, well at the time, I didn't really think anything of it ..."

"But?" he prompted.

"But, when we were waiting on line to check out, she got a call. I saw her check the number on her display and let it roll to voicemail. Whoever it was left a voicemail. When we were walking out of the store, she listened to it, and her whole face turned white, like all the blood drained out of it." Lynn's eyes were wide, and her voice was suddenly shaky. She picked up her glass and drained it before finishing her story. "We'd been planning to get some appetizers and drinks before my show, but she stood there staring at her phone for a minute and then said something about an emergency. She kept apologizing but said she had to go. She gave me a quick hug and then took off, almost running toward the subway station at the corner. And that was it. I figured I'd see her tomorrow at SoulCycle." Her eyes filled with tears. "But maybe I won't."

Seven

"Where to now?" I yawned and settled back into the passenger seat after we dropped Lynn off at her apartment. I was stuffed full of fresh pasta and good wine. My eyelids fluttered shut despite my best efforts. I struggled to lift them, but they were so heavy. Maybe a quick cat nap would help. I snuggled into the leather seat.

"I'm taking you home."

My eyes popped open and I sprang upright. I was suddenly wide awake. "What? No, we need to run down the phone call Helena got. Weren't you listening to Lynn? Your sister was definitely saying her goodbyes on Friday and—"

"Whoa, whoa, simmer down. Yes, I was listening. Trust me, I heard everything she said. I'm going to drop you off and then call my source at the wireless company that Helena used and ask her for a list of in-going and outgoing calls."

Oh, a source. It sounded so fancy. But still. I opened my mouth to argue. He took one hand off the steering wheel and held it up like a crossing guard.

"Let me finish. It's going to take a bit of time to get anything back from her cell phone. At least a day. Probably longer. In the meantime, we both have actual jobs to show up for in the morning. And *you* are asleep on your feet. So I'm taking you home, and you're going to meditate or whatever you do and then go to bed."

I undercut any response I might have made by un-leashing another giant yawn. He was right. I was ex-hausted. And, in the morning, I had not only Cate Whittier-Clay, but two other clients as well. I slumped back in defeat.

"Fine."

Of course, it *wasn't* fine. It was sensible and smart, but it definitely wasn't fine. Helena was out there, somewhere, possibly injured and bleeding, almost cer-tainly frightened. As he took the on-ramp onto FDR Drive, I took a deep breath and made one final push for going to the police. "You know, if you just reported her as a missing person, the police could be working on this, too. I'm not saying we should stop. I'm just saying we could run parallel investigations."

He gave me a sidelong look. "Parallel investiga-tions? Okay, Detective Field."

I grinned but stayed the course. "Victor, I'm serious."

"I know," he said with a heavy sigh. "And I hear you. I don't like it, but I think you're right. If Gabriel was looking for her, it sounds like he's already found her. Between the phone call and the blood ..."

I knew he couldn't finish the sentence. And I realized that, to him, getting law enforcement involved was a concession that his sister was already dead. My stomach lurched at the thought.

"No, on second thought, we should wait another day."

"Really?" he asked with a spark of hope that made my heart ache.

"Yeah, definitely. Let's give your source at the phone company some time and see what she can come up with before we get the fuzz involved."

"The fuzz?" A laugh bubbled up from his throat, which was totally my plan.

"Yep. Or the coppers, if you prefer."

Some of the dread seemed to seep out of the air in the town car. He grinned at my silliness, but he looked unconvinced about the idea of waiting to involve the authorities—even though he'd been so against it before.

"I don't know."

We drove in silence for a few minutes. He drummed his fingers on the steering wheel. *Rat-a-tat. Rat-a-tat.*

He was clearly mulling over my suggestion. I could almost see him weighing the benefit of keeping hope alive against getting closure.

He pulled over and parked in a loading zone near my building and turned to look at me. "Maybe you're right."

"I'm definitely right. Meet me back here tomorrow afternoon. I finish up with my last client at one o'clock. We'll see if we can't make some more progress."

A brief smile flashed across his face, but it faded almost instantly. He lowered his voice to a near whisper. "Thank you, Thyme. Thanks for helping me." He paused and swallowed hard. "I can't imagine doing this alone." He leaned across the front seat and searched my face with his warm, brown eyes. I could smell his woodsy cologne.

My insides felt all melty and gooey, sort of like the core of a toasted marshmallow.

"I'm not seeing anyone either," I yelped like an idiot. Then I unlatched my seatbelt and bolted from the car before he could respond.

Eight

All morning long, as I went through the motions with my clients, I was having an internal wrestling match with myself. Had I been in the right to convince Victor not to go to the police just yet?

I counted stretches, corrected forms, and reminded my clients to breathe. You'd be surprised how common it is for people to hold their breath while exercising. But the whole time I was training Cate, then Ella, then Marcy, I was completely wrapped up in the drama playing out in my whirring brain. It was a terrible habit, because, as I was quick to remind them, it always pays to be mindful of the task at hand. Whether that task was washing the dishes or performing asanas. You get more out of every activity if you're truly present.

In this case, though, it seemed I was incapable of taking my own advice. Even after I finished up with

Marcy and popped into the deli across the street from her office for a bowl of surprisingly tasty carrot-avocado soup, I ate mindlessly. By the time I was yanked back to reality by the sound of my spoon scraping the bottom of the empty bowl, I decided that we definitely needed to go to the police ASAP. I deposited my bowl and spoon in the dirty bin and marched off in the direction of my place, my mind made up.

Victor and his borrowed town car were waiting for me when I reached the corner. The Lincoln was parked dangerously close to a fire hydrant to my eye. Its driver leaned against the hood, legs and arms crossed.

"You're early," I said as a joined him beside the car.

"We've got lots to do," he chirped back.

Surprised by his cheery tone, I took a close look at him. He was positively vibrating with energy.

"What's going on? Did your source at the wireless company come through already?"

"Sort of," he said as he pulled open the passenger door and waved me toward the car. "Do you need to drop anything off at your place or can we go now? I'll fill you in on the way."

I slid into the passenger seat by way of answer. He shut the door behind me and jogged around to the driver's seat. As he started the engine I said, "Can I at least have a hint as to where we're headed?"

"Back to Helena's."

"Really?" I gnawed on my lower lip, glad that Sage wasn't around to see and call me out on it. She'd made it her mission in life to stop me from biting my nails; she didn't know I'd simply substituted chewing on my lip during trying times.

He glanced at me. "Something's on your mind. Spill it."

I shook my head. I wanted to hear what new development had him so excited before I decided to burst his bubble. "You first."

"My friend at the wireless company is still working to pull Helena's records, but she told me something that makes me think we may not even need her to."

I sat up a little straighter. "Really? What's that?"

"Helena's phone is still in her apartment." He swerved right, hard, to avoid a taxicab. I grabbed the door handle as we careened into the next lane over.

I waited until the crescendo of angry horns honking in our wake died down, then I asked, "They can tell where her phone is?" I realized it was a stupid question even as I formed the words.

They, whoever *they* are, can tell everything about a girl. It was downright creepy.

He nodded and kept his eyes on the traffic. "I asked my source to triangulate her location, but she didn't even have to. Helena's phone hasn't moved. It's sitting in her apartment, according to the GPS location. There've been no outgoing calls since Friday."

"Good thing her battery didn't die."

He laughed. "I'm pretty sure they can tell where a phone is even if it's turned off or the battery is dead."

I could tell from the cadence of his voice that he was really excited about this development. I chomped down harder on my lower lip and tried to silence the misgiving that was taking shape in my mind. Unfortunately, the thought ran around inside my mind like a hamster on a wheel—frantic, relentless, and noisy.

I cleared my throat. "Umm ... if Helena left of her own volition don't you think she'd have taken her phone with her?" I asked as gingerly as I could.

To my way of thinking, the fact that her phone was in the apartment was more proof that she was dead or—at best—had been abducted by her psycho ex-husband.

But he shook his head, rejecting my theory. "No, no. See, that's the thing. She got an upsetting call on Friday when she was with Lynn, right?"

"Yeah."

"If that call was from Gabriel, then she knew it was just a matter of time until he showed up at her place. She could have ditched the phone and taken off."

"Okay, that's plausible," I allowed, "but she also could've gone home and been ambushed by—"

"I know. Look, I just want to go to the apartment. I think it's worth checking to see if we can find the phone."

"Why's the phone so important to you if Helena doesn't have it?" I was still confused by his enthusiasm.

"If we can find the phone I don't need Mar—" he stopped himself before he blurted out his source's name. "I don't need my contact at the wireless company to take the risk of pulling Helena's call log and setting off whatever red flags that might set off. We'll have a log of all her incoming and outgoing calls right there on her phone. We'll be able to see who called her on Friday."

I could see the logic, but it also seemed as though he was grasping at straws. I mean, I guess when the options are your sister's dead or has decided to vanish without a trace, you grasped at whatever straws you could.

"Okay," I agreed lamely. I'd humor him for now.

"Did Cate say anything this morning?"

"Cate? You mean Cate Whittier-Clay?" I asked, blinking in confusion at the sudden change of topics.

"Yes. Did she mention Helena?"

I wasn't sure how to break it to him that his sister's employer viewed her, me, and everyone else who worked for her as entirely fungible. The new nanny, Janie, had shown up right on time and, as far as Cate was concerned, that was the end of the issue. Audra did seem to be missing Helena quite a bit, but Janie was taking special care to keep her busy and let her share her feelings about her old nanny. Audra would be okay in the end. I mean, as okay as a child raised in the hot-house flower environment of the Whittier-Clay pent-house could be.

I roused myself from my musing about Audra's up-bringing, when I realized he was waiting for an answer. "Ms. Whittier-Clay and I don't talk much," I explained. *That* was an understatement. Mainly she groaned and complained, and I offered motivation and encourage-ment. We didn't chitchat. Before I could give him the short version of Cate Whittier-Clay's philosophy re-garding making friends and influencing people, we reached Helena's apartment.

But instead of parking in the front, he snaked around to the bumpy back alley lined with rusty old dumpsters, trash cans, and weeds. He pulled over and parked on a piece of broken cement between a dented metal trash can a la Oscar the Grouch and a mostly dead thorny bush.

I gave him a look as he cut the engine. "I don't think this is a parking spot."

"I'm sure it's not," he agreed. "But, since we're about to commit a breaking and entering, I don't think a parking violation is our biggest concern."

"Hang on. You want to break into her apartment?"

"There's no other way in. We locked her door be-hind us when we left yesterday."

"At the risk of sounding obvious, you could take an-other shot at the super. Or start buzzing apartments again until we find another lonely person who wants to talk to a reporter."

"No." He shook his head. "I got a weird vibe from that super, and now that we know Gabriel might have tracked down Helena, I'm wondering if he bought that guy off. I don't want to risk tipping him off. And we don't have time to play reporter. Don't worry though, I've got a plan."

"Even so, you still shouldn't park the car right here."

He threw me a look. "Why not?"

"Don't you watch movies? Most serial killers are caught by observant meter maids. I assume the same applies to other criminals, too."

He rolled his eyes. "Wait here," he instructed.

I loitered beside the dumpster trying not to breathe too deeply while he moved the car down the alley and parked it a few buildings away.

~ ~ ~ ~ ~ ~ ~ ~ ~ ~

Victor's plan was—not to put too fine a point on it—a terrible one. I had plenty of time to consider its many shortcomings as I climbed. After he'd explained his idea, he boosted me in his hands so that I could reach the fire escape. Luckily for his deficient plan, I had enough upper body strength and flexibility to pull myself from the bottom rung to a position where I could scramble up the rungs like a monkey. It occurred to me that most sidekicks, including the long-limbed Lynn, would have had a hard time executing that move.

Sadly, though, my acrobatic maneuver was probably the best part of the plan because the rest of it involved me breaking into Helena's apartment through the window then buzzing Victor in. He'd said to walk straight through the apartment, hit the buzzer to let him in, and unlock her door. He planned to he'd loiter around in the alley until I was about halfway up and then head to the front door of the building to wait for me to buzz him in.

I twisted and glanced down behind me to confirm that he'd gone around to the front.

Whoa.

The ground looked very far away, and it occurred to me that jagged edges of cracked cement would hardly provide a pillowy cushion if I were to slip and fall. I gripped the metal ladder a little more tightly. Peeling paint flaked off in my hands and decades of dirt and grime fell off with it.

I moved up to the next rung and shifted my hands up as well. As I did, I felt something sticky.

Ugh.

I was almost afraid to look. Best-case scenario it would be disgusting New York City pigeon poop. I didn't really want to contemplate what the worst-case scenario would be. I paused in my climb to wipe my hand on the side of my pants, but when I pulled away from the railing I nearly lost my balance. My hand was covered, not with bird crap, but with brownish-red *stuff.* It looked like rust, but it felt viscous.

I climbed a few more rungs and another rusty spot caught my eye. I looked more closely at the metal ladder. There were rust-colored handprints on both sides spaced about six inches apart vertically. *Helena's blood.*

She must have used the fire escape to flee the apartment. Both my heart and my mind began to race as I pictured the scene: Gabriel had surprised her at the apartment; they'd struggled; she'd been injured but had managed to climb down the fire escape. My stomach lurched at the image.

I kept climbing and was careful not to put my hands in any more of the bloody spots. I ignored the bile rising in my throat. I couldn't afford to freak out now. When I reached the landing outside Helena's window, a hot breeze kicked up and blew a long strand of hair into my eyes. Reflexively I used my bloody right hand to push the hair away and caught an unmistakable whiff of chocolate.

I'd always heard that blood smelled like copper, but Helena's apparently smelled exactly like baking cocoa. Trust me. For all Rosemary's vegan, holistic, natural food philosophy, my oldest sister could make a mean dessert. I know the smell of chocolate.

I sniffed again. Definitely chocolate. Not quite believing what I was about to do, I cautiously raised my hand to my mouth and tentatively licked my index finger. Yep, chocolate. Bitter chocolate, probably cocoa powder, mixed with *something*, but not blood. I stood there for a long moment, trying to place the tang that cut through the cocoa taste and hoping it wasn't some dreadfully toxic pollutant.

I'd have to figure it out later. I had to break into the apartment and let Victor in. I reached into my pocket for the rubber mallet he'd given me.

Three quick taps, he'd told me. *Cover your face, but the glass should break inward.*

I didn't want to know how a *New York Times* reporter knew so much about breaking into an apartment. I eyed the bedroom window.

Here goes nothing, I thought. I raised the mallet and averted my face. Then I was struck by an idea: if Helena had climbed down the fire escape, which she clearly had, she wouldn't have been able to lock the window behind her. So unless Gabriel had locked it after she left, her bedroom window might still be open.

I returned the mallet to my pocket. It was worth a shot to at least check before I engaged in destruction of property. I put my fingers under the ledge and pushed up hard on the heavy, splintered frame. It groaned, but sure enough, gave way. Feeling more than a little delighted that my hunch had paid off, I scrunched up and lowered one leg into the apartment, balancing on the steam radiator under the windowsill.

I limboed inside. As I closed the window behind me I noticed another rust-red handprint that Victor and I hadn't seen yesterday. I hurried through the bedroom out to the kitchen. The buzzer was right where Victor had said I'd find it—on an intercom mounted near the door. I placed the mallet on the counter, hit the buzzer, then flipped the lock on the door to the right to disengage it for him. Then I hurried back down the hall to the bedroom. I had a hunch to run down before he got there.

I wanted to confirm my suspicion that it wasn't blood on Helena's bedding. I raced into the bedroom and pulled open the bifold closet doors. Then I lifted the comforter from the closet floor and inspected it. It still looked ghoulish and ghastly, as though it had been stained with evidence of a violent struggle, but now that I had theory about the so-called blood, I brought my face closer to the stain and sniffed. Beyond a shadow of a doubt, chocolate. And that tang? It sort of reminded me of ketchup.

Who would combine ketchup and chocolate? I shuddered. Then I thought back to the summer I was fifteen. Sage was seventeen and secretly dating Lucian, a college drama student spending his vacation doing summer stock at the community theater. The Seaside Playhouse had staged *Hamlet* that summer, and one weekend, before he and Sage had disappeared to swap spit in the barn behind our property, Lucian had shown us how to make blender stage blood on a budget. Ketchup and cocoa powder were the main ingredients.

I scraped at the stain with my fingernail and freed a chunk of the dried material. I took a cautious lick. Totally ketchup. I nearly gagged. I *loathe* condiments— all condiments, but ketchup and mustard in particular. Rosemary said it was because I was un-American. My culinary musings were interrupted by the front door opening.

I headed for the bedroom door with the comforter in hand to explain my discovery to Victor. Then I heard a male voice rumble low in Spanish. I froze. That definitely wasn't Victor's voice.

A second voice answered, also in Spanish, also not Victor. I began to shake and quiver and whirled my head around frantically, scanning the room in a panic as I considered my options. I could go back out through the window, but I was certain these men, whoever they were, would hear me pushing it open. My heart was thudding so loudly, I almost couldn't think. I gripped the fabric in my hand and got an idea.

I pulled the bedroom door closed silently then backed into Helena's closet and hooked my fingers through the slatted wood to pull the doors closed. Then I pulled the comforter over my head like a tent. The closet was dark, cramped, and hot. Under the comforter, I felt claustrophobic and cornered. And my heart was way too noisy. I scooted myself into the corner and hugged my arms around my knees, my eyes wide open in thick blackness, listening as hard as I could.

Heavy footsteps fell in the hallway. They stopped outside the bathroom. I heard voices echoing off the white tiles. The *skritch* as the hamper was pulled across the floor. Raised voices, alarmed I could tell even in a language I didn't understand. *They'd found the towel.* I shrank further back, pressing myself against the wall as if I might flatten myself into its surface if I just tried hard enough.

The footsteps resumed, the voices drew closer. I whimpered involuntarily and slammed my hand across my mouth. I squeezed my eyes shut and felt hot tears stream down my cheeks. *This was it. I was going to die in another woman's closet.*

Nine

As I cowered in the closet, waiting for something terrible to happen, I thought about my sisters.

Rosemary had taken down an armed murderer singlehandedly. Sage had crashed a golf cart through a plate glass window to save her boyfriend from yet *another* murderer. And here I was hiding under a comforter and trying not to whimper.

That's it. I was not going to spend what might be the last minutes of my life comparing myself to my sisters and coming up lacking. If I was going to die, I was going to die fighting.

Unfortunately, I didn't have a golf cart or even a rubber mallet, since I'd left that in the kitchen. I squinted around the closet in the darkness and tried to think of a plan. It occurred to me that if the intruders did open the closet they certainly wouldn't be looking up. While I may not have had a weapon, I was freakishly limber thanks to years of yoga and Pilates.

I tossed aside the comforter, stretched on my toes, and brushed the bottom of Helena's closet shelf with my fingertips. I looped my fingers around the wooden lip that edged the shelf and pulled myself up, flipping my legs over my head. My feet connected with the shelf and I swung myself up as if I were a trapeze artist. Then I crouched in a pile of scarves and hoped the shelf would hold my weight.

Then I waited. Like a cat on the savanna waiting for a gazelle to wander by, I waited, still and silent, poised to spring. The voices were getting louder, and I knew it was just a matter of moments before the men were in the bedroom. I focused on breathing evenly and slowly.

Cacophony erupted. Shouts, thuds, and banging sounded from just outside the bedroom door. My heart ticked up a notch and my legs began to quake. The noise grew louder, a door slammed, and the walls shook from the force. And then, just like that, the apartment was still and silent.

It could be a trap, I cautioned myself. I stayed hunched on the shelf, still shaking but refusing to be lured out of my hiding place and into a possible ambush. I told myself to count to one hundred. I got as far as thirty-seven when I heard the bedroom door creak open.

"Thyme?" a male voice called in a hoarse whisper.

How did they know my name?

I tensed and reminded myself to go down swinging, no matter what. I watched as the closet doors parted and opened. I lunged down from my perch and launched myself at the shape in the doorway. I hit him solidly, high on his neck, and he twisted. I clung to him and grabbed two fists full of his hair. He thrashed wildly. He stumbled into Helena's bed and let out a curse. I dropped to the floor in a crouch and planted myself on my left foot. I kicked out with my right and connected hard with his knee.

He bleated. "Thyme! Stop!" He crumpled into a heap on the bed.

Finally, my brain took over and I recognized Victor's voice. All the adrenaline that had flooded my body dissipated. I went limp with relief.

"Oh my gosh, are you okay?" I leaned over and inspected him with some concern.

He was rolling from side to side, with his right knee drawn up to his chest as if he were doing the *apanasana* pose. He groaned and pushed himself up to a seated position.

"What the hell?"

"I'm so sorry. There were two guys in here. I thought you were them."

He gave a half-laugh. "I know. I ran into them in the hallway near the bathroom. I didn't bother to ask who they were. I just drove my shoulder into the closer of the two and rammed him into the wall. His buddy pulled him up and they took off. But now I'm kind of wishing I'd let you handle them. I might have a permanent limp now."

I smiled sheepishly. "But how'd they get into the building?"

"You probably buzzed them in. Or they came in with someone else. I got to the door at that same time as someone with an armload of groceries. I held the door and followed her right in. I'd have been here sooner, but I helped her carry her bags to her apartment first."

Ever the gentleman.

"Did you get a good look at them?"

"The groceries? Some cat food. Lots of yogurt."

I sighed. "No. The guys."

"Two street punks. They were probably just trying doorknobs looking for an easy score."

"I don't think so. They were speaking Spanish. They looked in her hamper."

"Lots of folks speak Spanish."

I shot him a look. "Come on. Do lots of these Spanish speakers break into the apartments of missing women who have violent exes in South America and search their dirty laundry?"

He blanched then shook his head. "You think Gabriel sent them?"

"It stands to reason, doesn't it?"

"Not really. We speak Portuguese in Brazil."

"Really?" I felt like a dope.

"Yeah."

"Wait—why?"

"Because Pope Alexander the VI gave Brazil to the Portuguese. Now, enough with the history lesson. Are you sure it was Spanish you heard?"

"No," I admitted.

He dropped his head and cradled it in his hands while he digested the news. "Not that it's determinative. Most Brazilians know Spanish, as well. This is no good—if those guys are working for Gabriel ..."

I watched him for a minute, unsure of how to comfort him. Then I remembered the comforter. "It might actually be real good. I have to show you something." I reached into the closet and dragged the out the bedding.

He spread his fingers and looked through them. "That's not new. That's Helena's bloody comforter."

"It's not blood."

He raised his head and gave me a look that was a mixture of hope and disbelief. "What do you mean, it's not blood?"

"It's stage blood.   This is chocolate mixed with ketchup, Victor. Helena faked her death or injury or whatever."

"Thyme—"

"I'm telling you. Come with me." I took off for the kitchen without waiting to see if he'd follow. He did.

I looked around the galley. "Where's she keep her trash?"

"There." He pointed to the cabinet under the sink.

I yanked it open. A small, white, plastic trashcan was wedged under the pipes. I rocked it free and rifled through its contents. I placed the empty ketchup bottle and can of cocoa powder on the counter with a triumphant flourish.

"So?" he asked in a defeated voice. "This means nothing."

"Maybe nothing. You heard Lynn. Then suddenly, out of the blue, your sister needed to buy a blender. Do you think she had a daiquiri emergency? No, she needed it for this. And the new sheet set? I'm guessing she wanted to pick up a second set, so she wouldn't ruin her only ones." It's what I'd have done, at least.

"And she got a travel toothbrush." He stroked his chin as he considered it. Then he shook his head. "Lynn said she bought that stuff *before* she got the call that spooked her. Why would she be planning to fake her death before Gabriel called her?"

"You're assuming that call was from Gabriel. I don't know what went on to make her decide to mix up a batch of blender blood. But once we find her phone, maybe we'll be able to piece it together."

I returned the trash to the waste basket and washed my hands while Victor started to look for Helena's cell phone.

After watching him search through her couch cushions and paw through several drawers, I finally said, "Why don't you call it?"

"Call it. Right." He shook his head at himself and took out his phone.

"What kind of reporter are you, anyway? Please say not an investigative reporter," I cracked.

"I cover the financial markets," he mumbled as he pulled up Helena's contact information in his phone.

Bo-ring, I thought. Financial markets news sounded like something that would interest Sage and old, rich guys and no one else.

The chirping sound of a cell phone ringing interrupted my musing. The tinny ringtone was muffled and distant. We followed the sound back to Helena's bedroom, stopping so he could redial after her voicemail picked up. When the ringing resumed, it grew louder at first. But when we entered the bedroom, it faded again.

"Bathroom," I said.

We U-turned out of the room and headed toward the bathroom. It was definitely in here. The sound echoed off the tile walls. I pulled open the shallow, wall-mounted medicine cabinet over the sink. The contents were spare and organized, not the jumbled mess I'd expected. *Project much, Thyme?*

A pink iPhone sat on the bottom shelf, mostly concealed by a brighter pink tampon box.

"Found it." I removed it from its hiding spot and passed it to Victor. "I assume your sister doesn't typically store her phone with her feminine hygiene products?"

He shook his head, staring down at the phone in his palm. "She usually charges it beside her bed. Why would she hide it in here?"

"More support for my theory. She's on the run, Victor. She wanted to leave you a clue but she didn't want to just leave it in plain sight—in case Gabriel got here first."

He looked unconvinced. "Maybe." He started messing with the phone.

I figured he was trying to pull up her call log. But the fine hairs on my arms suddenly stood straight up and a chill ran through me.

"Come on, we can do that someplace else. Let's get out of here." My voice cracked with urgency and fear.

"What's wrong?"

"If Gabriel hasn't been here yet, he could be on his way. He could be in the stairwell right now. Or outside in the hall. Did you lock the door?" As if it mattered—a flimsy apartment door lock wasn't going to keep out a deranged police officer. I tugged on Victor's arm, almost frantic now. "Let's go."

He slipped the phone into his pocket. "You have a point."

But when we reached the hallway and I headed toward the kitchen, he pulled me back to the bedroom.

"What are you doing?"

"Let's go out the way you came in. Just in case you're right."

We hurried through Helena's bedroom. A flash of green and purple caught my eye. "Wait." I ran over and shoved the comforter back into the closet. As I did so, the hint of a thought danced through my brain. A wisp of smoke that said something was wrong or out of place. But then it vanished.

I frowned and filed the emotion away to think about later then joined Victor, who was waiting for me at the window. "Ladies first."

I threw one leg over the windowsill and straddled it for a moment to get my footing, then I slipped out onto the metal fire escape and clambered down the ladder as fast as I could. I didn't stop until I was crouched on the ground below.

~ ~ ~ ~ ~ ~ ~ ~ ~ ~

We sprinted through the alley to the waiting town car. I was half-convinced I could hear feet pounding after us. I had to force myself not to turn around and look behind me. Maybe the two guys who'd been in the apartment had hung around to catch us on our way out. Maybe Gabriel himself was running us down, a gun in hand, ready to take aim.

I lowered my head and poured on the speed, running flat out until I reached the shiny black car. Victor came up right on my heels, breathing hard. He popped the locks while he was still running and we threw open the doors and flung ourselves inside the car.

I leaned back against the seat and tried to catch my breath while he turned the key in the ignition. He peeled out of the alleyway, palming the steering wheel one-handed while he jammed his seatbelt clip into the buckle. I fastened my own seatbelt then eyeballed the speedometer and sent up a silent prayer to the universe.

"You make a pretty solid getaway driver for a financial reporter. And don't tell me it comes from your taxi driver days. Unless you did some off the books driving."

That earned me a chuckle. "Yeah, the commission didn't take too kindly to speeding. But this is how everyone drives in Rio. Fast."

I silently added Rio de Janeiro to my list of countries not to drive in. It's a long list.

"So what now?"

"We need to go someplace where we can review Helena's phone log safely." He glanced at me and put special emphasis on the word 'safely.'

"Are you saying we're in danger?"

"I'm saying I don't know. If those guys in the apartment are working for Gabriel, I'm sure they reported running into me. If they gave a halfway-decent description of me, he'll realize who I am. And, from there, it'll be easy enough for him to get a tail on me. Did they see you?"

"The guys?"

I shook my head. "No. I buzzed you—well, them—in and then went back to the bedroom to check out the comforter. When I heard them, I hid. So they know *someone* buzzed them in, but they don't even know that it came from Helena's apartment. I mean, right?" I thought what I was saying was the actual situation, but I also desperately needed to believe it. Even if it wasn't true. The near-miss in the apartment had rattled me.

"I think that's right. And they wouldn't have any reason to connect you to Helena or me just because you both worked for Cate Whittier-Clay."

I noted his use of the past tense but didn't mention it. He couldn't really believe his sister was dead—if he did, we'd be talking to the cops, not running around like idiots. "So, my place should be safe."

"Should be. For now, at least. But I don't want to risk taking you back there. If Gabriel is looking for me, I sure don't want to be the one to lead him to you."

"So, where can we go?" I really wanted to get off the street. I'd feel much safer inside some anonymous building. "Your office?"

He shook his head no. "I know a place."

Ten

The place he knew turned out to be the main branch of the New York Public Library—the one in Manhattan with the famous, majestic lions Patience and Fortitude guarding the steps. We didn't stop to admire the statues, though. He was in a hurry.

He led me to the mixed-use research rooms on the first floor and poked his head into one room after another, looking for a vacant one. They were all buzzing with activity, except for the periodical research room where one dark-skinned girl with a pile of long, heavy braids coiled into a tall bun on the top of her head was poring over a stack of magazines. It would do. She glanced up when we walked in, then immediately returned to her reading.

Victor picked the table furthest from her and pulled out a chair for me. I sat down and waited while he carried over a chair from the other side of the table. He placed it beside mine with the softest of thuds. The woman didn't look up.

He removed Helena's phone from his pocket and sat down. We both leaned in to see the screen, so close that our foreheads touched. I pulled back slightly, startled by the contact.

"Here." He handed me the phone and pulled out his notebook. I scrolled through the calls slowly while he jotted down the numbers and provided occasional commentary in a low voice. We started with her outgoing calls, beginning with her last call and working our way back. She'd made a call Friday evening just before eight p.m. to a number with a 215 area code. The call had lasted three minutes.

"That's a Philadelphia number," he breathed near my ear. "I don't know who she knows in Philly."

"It could be a mobile number that the person just never changed," I cautioned. Even though Rosemary was now in Los Angeles and Sage was in South Carolina, they'd kept their Boston and Washington, DC cell phone numbers.

He frowned but nodded his agreement. "Could be. Let's move on."

He recognized the next call as being to Lynn's number, a brief call placed just before Helena and Lynn met at the nail salon. Probably a call to let her friend know she was on her way.

The call before that was to a New York number that neither of us could place. He jotted it in his notebook and made a notation of the time and length.

That was it for Friday. Three outgoing calls, one to her girlfriend. Not much to go on. I scrolled further.

Thursday night she'd called Victor's number. He said they'd confirmed their brunch plans. There were no other Thursday calls on her log. I wasn't particularly surprised. I spoke on the phone with my sisters pretty regularly, but I mainly texted everyone else unless I had a specific reason to call instead. I was about to share this thought with Victor, when the woman with the braids suddenly pushed back her chair and rose to her feet.

My entire body tensed, expecting her to shout for Gabriel, who would then emerge from the stacks. He'd crash into us, grab the phone, and take off—maybe leaving his henchmen behind to rough us up. The woman raised her arms over her head, and I opened my mouth to shout a warning, but she rolled her neck from side to side, then cracked her back. Her stretch completed, she returned to her seat and picked up where she'd left off reading.

I exhaled in relief. Victor gave me a concerned look.

"Sorry. I'm just a little on edge, I guess," I whispered.

"I noticed." He smiled and placed his hand on the middle of my back in a gesture I'm sure was intended to soothe me. But his skin was warm, even through my tee shirt I could feel his hand heating my back. The gentle pressure of his touch was distracting.

I wriggled a bit and he pulled his hand back.

"I'm okay. Let's stay focused."

"Sure thing."

"Does your sister text?"

He nodded. "Yeah. I was thinking the same thing. She'll probably have more text messages than calls, but let's just check out the incoming calls first. We know whoever spooked her called Friday evening and left her a voicemail."

I pulled up her incoming log. We skimmed dozens of missed calls from the past four days—several from the nannying service, one placed Monday morning that I recognized as coming from Cate's assistant's number, and then call after call from Victor, trying to track her down after she didn't show up for brunch on Sunday. I scrolled further. She had six missed calls on Saturday, all from the same number.

I glanced up at him. I didn't even need to ask the question. I could tell from the furrow creasing his forehead that he didn't recognize the number. Without realizing what I was doing, I reached out and smoothed my fingertips over the worry lines.

He blinked and I pulled my hand back. "Sorry."

He shook his head and fixed me with a look I couldn't quite read. "Don't be."

We stared at each for a long moment. The silence stretched from normal to socially acceptable to downright weird. I cleared my throat and turned my attention back to the call log.

"Your skin's soft." He said it in a low whisper, almost as if he didn't want me to hear him. So I pretended not to.

I gnawed on my lower lip and pointed at the screen. "Look at this." The same number that had called six times on Saturday also placed multiple calls to Helena's number on Friday evening and well into the night. I tallied them softly. "Eight missed calls. Plus six the next day. Someone tried to get a hold of her fourteen times in two days and then just ... stopped? That's crazy."

"It's only crazy if the caller didn't eventually get in touch with her," he said.

Good point.

"Do you know the area code?" I asked.

"No, but this one moves to the top of the list for my friend at the mobile company."

"Or we could, you know, Google it. Or just call the number."

He stared at me as if I'd sprouted a second head. "Call it?"

"It's just an idea," I said defensively.

"It's a great one. Let's finish this up and then go do that."

In his excitement he nearly shouted, which earned us a really nasty glare from the woman at the table. 'Sorry,' I mouthed.

"The only other entry is a voicemail that came in about ten minutes before the first call from that number." He leaned over my shoulder and pointed. "And look at the time. That's the call she got when she was in Target."

Before I had a chance to respond he was dragging me toward the staircase and out of the library. As soon as we stepped out onto the wide marble stairs, he gestured to a sheltered spot behind a column.

"Let me have the phone."

I handed it over. "What are you doing?"

"I'm putting it on speaker so we can listen to her voicemail messages. We've got the bastard now." He fumbled with the phone for a moment.

I realized I was holding my breath and exhaled. The automated voice announced, "You have no new messages. You have no saved messages."

"She deleted it." My voice sounded flat and heavy to my own ears. I couldn't believe she deleted the message that had set off whatever events had followed.

"She deleted it," he echoed in an equally dull voice. His shoulders slumped toward the ground as if he were melting.

I didn't know what to say. I wrapped my arms around him in a gentle hug.

Eleven

We walked to the car in silence. Victor pocketed the parking ticket tucked under the windshield wipers in silence. And we drove for several long blocks in silence. Our timing was apparently as bad as our luck, because we caught every red light on our route. It was like the reverse of riding an urban wave. It was a jerky, slow, no-fun urban lazy river.

As we sat (in silence) at what must have been the forty-seventh traffic light, my stomach suddenly filled the conversational void with a horrible, deafening growl. It sounded like a pissed-off bobcat.

He turned to me wide-eyed. "Was that you?"

I swallowed a giggle and shrugged. "I guess I'm hungry."

"You guess? Hang in there. I know a good Cuban joint not too far from here—over in Hell's Kitchen. I'll buy you a sandwich so long as you promise not eat my arm on the way."

I put on my best serious face. "I make no promises. Especially if you're going to take the scenic route."

"Careful what you wish for, Thyme." And with that, he flashed a grin and peeled left, cutting off a Prius in the process. I closed my eyes and visualized a pork sandwich and a cold beer. Maybe I could distract myself from his reckless driving with thoughts of food. If not, at least I'd die happy when we crashed.

I opened my eyes when we screeched to a stop in a city parking lot and I pitched forward. He extended his arm to prevent me from smashing into the dashboard.

"You drive like a lunatic," I mumbled as I unbuckled my seat belt and gathered up all the crap that had spilled out of my purse all over the floor during our joyride.

"Here, let me help you." He leaned across the front seat and reached for my wallet.

"Thanks."

I took it and shoved it in my bag then started to sit up. Suddenly, he was pushing my head down, forcing me into a folded-over position.

"Hey!" I yelped.

He covered my back with his body, hunching over me.

"Shhh." His mouth was right beside my ear.

I wriggled underneath him and tried to push him off. "What the hell?"

"Be still. And be quiet, would you? Those two guys from Helena's apartment are walking through the lot, headed toward us."

I stopped moving. "Are you sure it's them?" I hissed in a whisper.

"Pretty sure. The taller one has his hand in his jacket pocket, like he has a weapon maybe."

"A gun?"

"I don't know. And I don't intend to find out."

I turned my head to try to face him. "What are you going to do?"

"Drive like a lunatic. Can you get down on the floor all the way?"

"Sure."

He eased his weight off me and fumbled with the keys. I slid down to the passenger side floor and rolled myself into a tight child's pose with my head down. The car rocketed to life and lurched into motion. I squeezed my eyes shut.

As the sedan careened out of the parking lot, I heard male voices shouting. Suddenly, a *crack* filled the air. In the same instant, the sedan's back window shattered. Glass shards rained down into the passenger compartment. My heart leaped into my throat and I peeked up at Victor. He ducked his head below the level of the now-broken window and gunned the engine.

Great. Now we were speeding along a New York City street without even looking. I braced myself for the inevitable impact, but it never came.

After a moment, he raised his head and returned to a normal seated position. I watched him check the rearview mirror.

"We lost them," he assured me.

I pulled myself up to the passenger seat and buckled in. "For now."

"For now," he agreed.

As if it understood that the pulled pork sandwich was off the table, my stomach chimed in with a half-hearted rumble.

~ ~ ~ ~ ~ ~ ~ ~ ~ ~

I gnawed unenthusiastically on the stick of spiced turkey jerky. Victor chewed his peanuts glumly. We huddled side by side on the metal park bench, eating our bodega snacks and drinking our overpriced bottled waters.

"I will have to take you to Cuba Libra some time. When this is all over," he mused.

I blinked at the notion that we'd be in one another's lives after *this* and tore off another piece of cured meat with my teeth. After I swallowed, I took another sip of water and said, "Hey, don't worry. This isn't even close to the worst lunch date I've ever had."

He turned to face me. "I sincerely hope you're joking."

"If only. One of my clients set me up with her co-worker's brother."

"How bad was it?"

"He took me to a free lunch buffet at a strip club."

He grimaced. "Oooff."

"Yeah. I guess people don't go there for the food? I still don't know if I was eating chicken or fish."

He snorted and nearly choked on his peanuts. "You ate the food?" he wheezed between coughs.

I pounded his back with my fist until he raised his hand to stop.

"I'm okay." He wiped his eyes with the back of his hand and gulped his water. "I can't believe you ate the food."

"Let's move on. What's our next step?" I asked, mainly to change the subject to something, anything, less embarrassing.

Afraid that Gabriel or his minions had put a tracking device on the Lincoln, we'd ditched the town car on a side street. Victor had called the car's owner to explain and apologize—or at least, I assume that had been the gist of the conversation. He'd spoken in rapid-fire Spanish (or Portuguese, for all I knew) and I'd only picked up a handful of words. We'd put at least a dozen city blocks between us and the car before he finally gave into my whining about my hunger pangs and had stopped at the little bodega where we'd bought the first foodstuffs we'd seen and hurried out of the store.

He shrugged. "Aside from the part where we have no vehicle and you're enjoying your second-worst lunch date, the plan hasn't changed." He pulled Helena's phone from his pocket and powered it on. "Let's run down these phone numbers." I reached into my tote bag and took out his reporter's notebook, which had ended up mixed in with my stuff in the chaos of being shot at.

I handed him the notebook. "What about the police?"

We'd already fought this battle once, right after we'd abandoned the car. But I was hoping that, once adrenaline and abject terror were no longer coursing through his veins, he'd come around to see the wisdom of leaving the search for his sister in the hands of professionals. Armed professionals. With handcuffs, even. I mean, we couldn't just continue to traipse around the city being trailed by gunmen.

He puffed out his cheeks and exhaled slowly. "Look, I'll understand if you want to leave. The situation has clearly gone from risky to extremely dangerous. And, if you want to go to the cops, I won't stop you. But I'm not giving up. I'm going to keep looking for Helena. I don't have time to waste cooling my heels in a police station and repeating the story for a parade of uniforms."

I studied his face but didn't respond. His dark brown eyes looked tired and scared but resolved.

He went on, "I'll never be able to thank you for helping me as much as you have. But I can't guarantee your safety going forward. You should walk away from me right now."

I pictured myself standing up, pitching my water bottle in the nearby recycling bin, and finding my way to the nearest subway station. It would be the safest thing to do. Understandable. Smart, even.

Instead, I leaned across the park bench and pressed my mouth against his. He froze for a moment then kissed me back—an urgent, searching kiss. My hands found his head and I laced my fingers together in his thick, curly hair.

Twelve

We walked, holding hands in that self-conscious way people do when they don't yet know how their fingers best fit together, until we found a rundown Chinese restaurant with a blinking open sign, sticky tables, and a bored, surly staff. Even I, consumer of a strip club lunch buffet, knew this wasn't the kind of restaurant you opted for over a jerky stick, but it was empty, quiet, and got us off the street and away from prying eyes. At this point, I didn't even know what neighborhood we were in, other than it was someplace I'd never been.

We seated ourselves, squeezing into the booth beside one another. I could almost hear my sisters mocking us for sitting next to each other rather than across the table from one another. Rosemary, in particular, viewed it as a telltale sign of a new romance. Thinking about myself engaged in a romance with Victor got me all flustered and my face warmed up. I could tell I was blushing, which just made me blush more furiously. Victor rested his hand on my thigh under the table. That didn't help.

A grumpy waiter made his way over to us and didn't seem remotely surprised by our request for "just jasmine tea," which confirmed my impression of the food. He strode away without another word and returned almost immediately. He slammed the pot and two small teacups down on the table along with the bill then disappeared without ceremony.

Victor placed a twenty-dollar bill on top of the check while I poured the tea.

"I probably have a five," I offered, reaching for my wallet.

He shook his head. "A twenty buys us whatever good will that guy has, which is probably not much."

"Maybe his shoes are too tight."

Victor laughed. "Maybe. But either way, it doesn't look like he rakes in the tips at this joint. Let's hope he'll be grateful enough to keep his mouth shut if anyone comes looking for us."

My brain stopped replaying our kiss and focused on his words. "You think Gabriel can track us down here? I thought you said those guys probably tagged the car while we were in your sister's apartment?" The memory of being shot at supplanted the memory of making out, and my pulse rate ticked up a couple notches for all the wrong reasons.

"That's my working theory. But until my friend confirms whether he found a tracking device on his Lincoln, we shouldn't assume that's how they caught up with us."

I stared at him. "How else could they have known where we were?"

He shrugged. "Who knows?" He dumped a packet of artificial sweetener into his cup and swirled it around with a somewhat-clean spoon.

I sipped mine, unadulterated. I don't care for sweet drinks. And even if I did, I wouldn't use the other spoon to save my life. It was coated with what appeared to be rice and plum sauce that had gone through a dishwasher and gelled onto the utensil.

He flipped open his notebook and picked up Helena's phone. "Let's call the Philly number first."

"Are you sure?" We didn't know the voice on the other end would be a friend or a foe.

"I think so. Helena called this number and talked for three minutes, so presumably it belongs to someone she wanted to speak with before she vanished. We'll call from her phone. Hopefully whoever it is will recognize her number and pick up."

It was a long shot, but I didn't have a better idea, so I nodded and drank my tea.

He picked up the phone and hit redial on the menu. I held my breath and strained to listen. After a moment, I heard the faint, but distinctive, sound of the three, short "this number has been disconnected" tones followed by the electronic voice recording advising us that the wireless caller we were trying to reach was not available. Victor ended the call and shook his head in disgust.

"Another dead end. Just our luck."

I sipped my tea. "You don't think it's really just bad luck, though, right?"

He tilted his head in my direction. "Meaning?"

"Meaning it would be an awfully big coincidence for someone to disconnect their line between Friday night and today. Unless ..."

"Unless what?"

"Unless it was prearranged with Helena. Or unless the person just set up an intercept to block Helena's number."

"Can you do that?"

I threw up my hands. "Don't ask me. Probably. Your friend at the phone company should know. Ask her."

"I will. But I only want to call her once. Let's work through as much as we can and make a list of questions and tasks for her." He scribbled in his little notebook, and I choked back a laugh.

His eyes met mine. "What's so funny?"

"You just remind me of my sister, that's all."

He marked his spot with his pen and closed the notebook. "Which one?"

"Sage. She's an ... well, she used to be a forensic accountant. She's a nanny now. But she has that very fastidious, precise accountant attitude. She'd totally save all her questions for one call."

"It's not *that* weird," he insisted defensively.

"It is for a reporter. I thought you guys were sort of scattered, digging out notes from deep within piles of paper, all stained with coffee rings and stuff."

He rolled his eyes at me. "Stereotype much?"

"Ah, I forgot. You're a *financial* reporter. Of course you cross your Ts and dot your Is."

"You say that like it's a bad thing."

"It's not," I assured him. "It's just pretty foreign to me. I was raised in a fairly loosey-goosey manner. I think Sage's detail-oriented nature and love for mathematics and finance was her way of rebelling against our hippie upbringing."

"What did they do? For work, I mean?"

"They used to own an eco-resort. Now they don't."

"Small business owners? I think they might have had more business savvy than you give them credit for."

Yeah, until they didn't, I thought.

I changed the subject. "Let's Google the number. Start there, at least."

He kept his eyes locked on mine for a few seconds longer, as if he were willing me to talk about my family. But I just gazed back at him blankly until he blinked then looked away.

"Right," he mumbled. He rested his sister's phone on the table and pulled out his own.

He typed in a Google search with his thumbs then swiped past the first several hits, grumbling about the bait-and-switch results that required a credit card to get the full report. I smiled to myself; I shared that pet peeve.

I refilled my cup from the little ceramic teapot, careful not to touch the sticky, plasticized tablecloth. While he drilled down into the results, I drank my tea and fought the urge to search out the world's largest container of thyme oil.

Thyme oil happens to be a natural sanitizer. There were no alcohol-based gels for the Field family. We made our own. From thyme grown right in on little seaside plot of land. Anyway, my skin was crawling, and I vowed to not to glance at the posted grade by the front door on my way out and to never, *ever* look up the restaurant on the health department's website. I was sure I didn't want to know how many violations this joint had racked up.

I peered over Victor's shoulder at his results. "Mia Kim. She's the owner of the phone?"

"Apparently."

"Does her name ring a bell?"

He rubbed his hand across his lips. "No." He shook his head and repeated the word. "No."

Before I could tell him that I knew he was lying, the bell above the restaurant's front door tinkled and I shifted my gaze to the front of the building to see the poor sucker who'd decided to eat here. It wasn't a lone diner. Two men crowded into the narrow entryway. Something about them made me uneasy. I don't know if it was their demeanor or their appearance or what. But I tensed as soon as I spotted them.

Then the taller of the two called to a waiter on the far side of the room, who disappeared around the corner without acknowledging him. At the sound of his voice, a shock of recognition ran through me. I scooped up our personal belongings from the table and threw them in my purse. I grabbed Victor's wrist, wrenched it hard, and pulled him down alongside me as I slid under the table.

"Ow," he yelped, trying to shake himself free of me.

"Shh, shh." I covered his mouth with my other hand and jammed my mouth right next to his ear. "They're here. The guys from the apartment. I don't think they spotted us."

His eyes widened with comprehension and fear, and I slowly removed my hand. We crouched there wordlessly in the cramped space and waited. I strained to hear over the impossibly loud thudding of my heart, like the bass line in a song. I could just make out low voices, growing louder, as footsteps neared our table.

I held my breath as two pairs of running shoes stopped beside the table. In my mind, I pictured what they were seeing. Tea for two. Cash to cover the check on the table.

"*Eles se foram.*" A guttural voice, almost a growl.

"*Desaparecido,*" came the reply. The disgust needed no translation.

After an interminable minute, the feet moved away, continuing on to the back of the restaurant. I figured they'd check the bathrooms, maybe peek into the kitchen and ask a waiter if he'd seen us, and then leave.

Hang tight, Thyme, I told myself. *Just a few minutes more.*

Beside me, Victor squeezed my hand—a gesture of solidarity, or maybe reassurance. The footsteps returned, passing our table, headed back toward the front. Just a few more steps and they'd be out of the restaurant, away from us. We'd be safe.

That's when the rat ran across my thigh.

~ ~ ~ ~ ~ ~ ~ ~ ~ ~

I held the napkin to Victor's hand, applying gentle pressure to stop the bleeding. "I'm really sorry I bit you," I apologized for the umpteenth time.

It was true. I felt awful. But when he clamped his hand over my mouth to keep me from screaming that blasted rodent turned around and ran right back across my lap going the other direction. There's no other way to put it—I freaked out. Apparently my teeth came down hard on the soft, fleshy webbing between his thumb and forefinger.

And, man, was Victor ever a *bleeder.* He'd toughed it out under the table until the bad guys had left the building and even waited an extra minute or two after the bell announced their departure.

But once they were definitely clear of the restaurant, he'd jumped up, holding his arm aloft. Blood squirted everywhere. Our waiter raced over to give us the stink-eye but locked in on the Jackson still sitting on the table and offered assistance instead. He'd even procured a reasonably cleanish cloth napkin before he pocketed the bill and glided away.

Victor shook his head. "What are you, part vampire? Your teeth are like razors."

I opened my mouth to apologize yet again but he waved his hand.

"I'm kidding. Jeez, Thyme. It's no big deal. Although"—he paused here to lower his voice to a husky near-whisper—"I think I prefer when you put your mouth to ... other uses."

I caught myself staring at his lips and would have kissed him again right then and there, but the memory of the men in the restaurant was too fresh. This wasn't the time for canoodling.

"Were those guys speaking Portuguese?"

His face darkened. "Yes."

"What did they say?"

"They came here expecting to find us. The first guy said, 'they're gone.' The other one said, 'vanished.' How did they know we were here? I don't get it."

I furrowed my brow and thought. The men had been tracking us since we'd left Helena's apartment, but how? After the incident in the parking lot, we'd thought maybe they'd put a tracking device on the car while we were in the apartment, but we'd left the car miles away from the restaurant. It made no sense.

"I don't know," I admitted. "It's almost like they put a tracker on one of *us*. But they didn't see me in the closet. When you ran into them in the hallway, did one of them slip something into your pocket or something?"

He shook his head and reached his good, unbitten hand into his pocket and pulled out Helena's phone. "Nope. And my phone and my wallet are in your bag. You have my notebook, too, right?"

I didn't answer him. I was focusing on the gleaming rectangle in his hand.

"Thyme?"

"Sorry," I said slowly, finally pulling my eyes away from his sister's phone to meet his gaze. "We have to dump Helena's phone."

Victor blanched. "Of course. Her phone. They're tracking us through her phone." He pushed the device to the other side of the table, as if he couldn't get far enough away from it."

"But if they can do that, it means *they* have a source at the wireless company, right?"

"Yep. Or, more likely, Gabriel hooked up with a local police department or some other law enforcement agency. I don't think he has the juice to pull any strings inside TeleVantage directly. But he could have gotten a brother in blue to help him out, officer to officer, under some pretense."

We stared at the phone for a long moment.

Then Victor signaled for our waiter, who was loitering just outside the kitchen no doubt waiting for us to leave already. The guy scurried over.

"Thanks for your help," Victor said as he folded the blood-stained napkin into a neat square. "I'll dispose of this for you, okay? Just point us toward your trash."

The man considered for a moment, weighing his options. Even a rat-infested dive probably drew the line at reusing linens that had been exposed to a customer's bodily fluids—I hoped. After a few seconds, he shrugged. "Sure. Follow me."

I grabbed my purse and the phone from the booth. We trailed him through the swinging door into the kitchen. A bored line cook looked up from clipping his nails. The dishwasher, wearing earbuds, bopped along to whatever music he was listening to, oblivious to our presence. Our waiter led us through the space to a set of metal doors.

"Dumpster's out back," he said pointing to the door.

We pushed open the heavy door and stepped out onto a concrete loading dock. The Dumpster sat just below near the curb. I crouched and jumped down to the ground. Victor followed suit. He opened the rusted Dumpster lid and tossed in the bloodied napkin then gestured toward me.

"Get rid of the phone."

I shook my head. "I have a better idea. Let's send it for a ride."

Two buildings to the right, a beer truck idled as its driver wheeled a pallet of kegs up a ramp, making a delivery to a neighboring establishment. I jogged over and slipped Helena's cell phone into the open truck. It skidded across the metal floor and landed in the back corner.

With any luck, Gabriel's goons would waste their time chasing the Budweiser guy from borough to borough while we figured out our next steps. I was feeling pretty clever when I rejoined Victor behind the Chinese restaurant.

"Now what?" I asked.

"Now we regroup. It'll be dark soon. We should get off the street until we have a plan. It's safe to assume those goons are working for Gabriel. He'll be able to find me easily. And if he ties you to Helena through the Whittier-Clays ..."

I stared at him, feeling exponentially less clever by the second. "I'm not sure I follow. What are you saying? It's not safe for me to go home?"

Victor raised his shoulders. "I don't know. But I do know I'd hate myself if something happened to you. So, I think we should find a hotel for the night. And you should cancel your client appointments for tomorrow. Just in case."

Thirteen

We walked for a long time, taking a circuitous route to the subway station on Forty-Ninth Street. We took the N Train to Barclays Center. During the ride, which lasted about a half an hour, we talked in low voices, forehead to forehead, sketching out our next moves as we swayed from side to side with the car.

After Union Square, two seats opened up next to each other and we snagged them. I pulled out my phone and texted my next day's clients an apologetic cancellation, citing a nasty bout of food poisoning. Then I sent Rosemary and Sage a long text, explaining that I was about to go dark for a day or two. I told them not to worry if they couldn't reach me. Then I removed the battery from my phone and stowed it in my purse. I knew the warning text was useless. If anything it would probably make my sisters ramp up their level of concern, but I couldn't just drop off the face of the earth with no notice. I'd have their hides if they ever pulled a stunt like that.

Beside me, Victor made whatever excuses he needed to make at work in a text of his own and then took out his phone's battery. Neither of us were TeleVantage customers, but if Gabriel had the capacity to track Helena's cell phone, there was no reason to think he couldn't somehow get ahold of our phones' locations, too.

And just like that, we were off the grid. Or, as off the grid as one could be taking New Your City public transportation to a hipster, boutique hotel in Brooklyn. I mean, sure, we weren't exactly camping in a state forest and catching fish with our hands or anything. But without cell phones, we couldn't order GrubHub or call for an Uber or anything. For two Manhattanites, our current situation was positively rustic. Primitive, even.

I giggled to myself about the absurdity of it all. He shot me a curious look then squinted at the station name that flashed by out the window.

"That was Canal Street. The next stop's us," he said.

We stood and fought our way through the crush of NYU students who'd boarded right after we'd found seats. We squeezed out the doors when they opened and hurried along the platform to the stairs.

The hotel was about half a mile from the station. We covered the distance in just under ten minutes, heads down, walking fast. I knew we looked like two ordinary New Yorkers, always in a hurry as we strode along the street.

But I felt anything but ordinary. I was on edge, half-expecting two Portuguese men to jump out from every doorway that we passed and gun us down in the middle of the sidewalk. I felt disconnected, adrift, and anonymous as a result of the simple act of turning off my phone. And, if I'm being honest, I felt a little shiver of anticipation at the thought of holing up in a hotel with Victor. I mean, I'd be getting my own room, but there was something undeniably intimate about disappearing together for the night. And he was a *great* kisser.

I shook my head at the silly tangent. Beside me, Victor said, "What?"

"Nothing."

"Are you sure you're up for this?" he stopped and pulled me out of the flow of foot traffic. We huddled against the side of a nondescript red brick building.

"I'm sure."

"Because if you're not—"

"I said I'm sure." I waved away his worry.

He leaned in close and smiled, his mouth just a few inches from mine. "Good," he breathed. "I'm getting used to having you around."

His impossibly long eyelashes brushed his cheek-
bones as he glanced down for a moment then reached
out and smoothed my hair back from my face. I tried to
ignore my fluttering heartbeat as he covered my mouth
with a searching kiss. *Yep, we were definitely going to
need separate rooms.*

~ ~ ~ ~ ~ ~ ~ ~ ~ ~

"I'm terribly sorry," the desk clerk said in a nasal,
not-even-remotely-sorry tone, "but I don't have two
rooms available for this evening. There's a three-day
craft beer symposium being held at the brewery
around the corner, and we're booked solid. There *was* a
cancellation this morning, so I can offer you one room.
A deluxe king with a partial view." He shifted his gaze
from Victor to me and back to Victor again, unable to
keep his mild amusement off his face.

Victor looked at me and raised both eyebrows, as if
to say, "It's your call."

I was hungry and tired of walking around. I didn't
want to schlepp to the next hipster boutique and hope
for better luck. I wanted to raid a minibar for some
overpriced booze and nuts and collapse into bed—
alone.

"Is there a couch or anything in this deluxe room?" I asked, even though I suspected I knew the answer.

"No. But I can have housekeeping bring up a cot."

Yippee, a cot.

"Sounds great," I said, flashing a smile that no doubt looked nearly as fake as it felt.

The clerk followed suit with an insincere grin of his own. "Excellent."

He clacked away at his computer keys and processed my credit card while I checked out the lobby. TripAdvisor had described the design as "open, airy post-industrial meets mid-century," which apparently translated into lots of metal, glass, and wood. No fabrics. Backless chairs. And a dimly lit hotel bar.

"Your card, Ms. Field." He passed my credit card and driver's license, along with a recycled paper key card sleeve, across the counter. He pointed to the room number he'd scribbled on the sleeve in black marker and rattled off the directions to the elevator, which was plainly visible just to the right of the entrance to the bar.

I shoved my card into my wallet and handed Victor one of the two key cards. We set off across the vast lobby toward the elevator bank.

"Have a nice evening," the clerk called in a strangled voice, as if he we were choking back a laugh.

"Is it just me or is that guy a weirdo?" I asked.

"He thinks we're having an affair," Victor explained. "Or at least a quickie."

I blinked, startled, and felt my skin start to heat up. "Why on earth would he think that?"

He shrugged and jabbed the elevator call button. "We show up after five p.m. with no reservation and no luggage; you have a New York address on the ID you showed him; and, well, you're pretty cute. Why wouldn't he think that?"

Pretty cute? I suddenly felt all of ten years old. *Why do guys think girls want to be described as pretty cute? I mean, I guess it beats smelly and humorless, but, jeez.* I pushed the thought out of my mind.

"Wait. I asked for two rooms. Who gets two rooms to have a ... um ... quickie?"

"Paranoid cheaters, maybe? How should I know?"

The amber light over the elevator to our right blinked to life and the doors parted. As we stepped inside the empty car, I said, "So you've never dated a married woman?"

He stared at me, his lips slightly parted.

I pushed the button for our floor and said, "Oh, gosh, don't answer that. I'm sorry, that was a really rude question. I used to do research into gender differences regarding monogamy. I asked all sorts of inappropriate, personal questions. Old habit," I explained, mortified at myself, as the words cascaded out of my mouth like a verbal waterfall.

He furrowed his brow but nodded, like my explanation made at least a modicum of sense. "Monogamy research, huh?"

"Well, human behavioral psychology, but yeah."

We reached the fifth floor and the elevator juddered to a stop with a loud thunk. He trailed me out into the hallway.

"To answer the question posed, no, I've never been involved with a married woman," he said to my back.

I didn't respond.

We reached our room and I inserted the key card into the reader. Nothing happened. I yanked it out and tried again. Still nothing. I huffed out an irritated breath. Victor reached over and plucked the card out of my fingers, flipped it around, and stuck it in the reader. The green light blinked and the metallic click sounded.

We were in.

I pushed open the door and walked inside. To say that the deluxe king room was small was to vastly overstate its size. It was teeny. The bed dominated the room to the point where I thought Victor might have to squeeze between the bed and the dresser sideways. I could barely fit, and I wasn't exactly broad-shouldered. Where on earth would a cot go?

I sidled through the narrow space and pulled open the drapes. "Look at that. There actually *is* a view."

Victor made his way to the window set into the exposed brick wall and peered over my shoulder. A sliver of the East River peeked out from between the buildings across the street, gleaming with reflected light, like a dark silk ribbon. Beyond it, Manhattan's skyline rose in the dusk.

"What a city," he breathed.

I leaned back and rested my head on his chest. He pulled me closer. I relaxed into his arms, ready to unwind after the day we'd had. Then I remembered Mia Kim. I shrugged out of his grip, twisted my neck, and stared up at him.

"Who's Mia Kim?"

His face closed like a door. "I told you, I don't know the name. She must be a friend of Helena's. I never met her."

I backed up another step and bumped into the rough surface of the brick wall. I kept my eyes glued on his. "I know you're lying."

He jerked his head back like I'd slapped him.

"I'm not ..."

I tilted my head and arched my left eyebrow only— a talent my sisters envied and had been trying to replicate, without success, since we were kids. I said nothing.

"I didn't ..."

He took a small step backward and lowered himself until he was sitting at the foot of the bed.

"How?" he asked.

"How do I know you're lying?"

He shook his head sadly from side to side. "Yeah."

"There's a checklist of common lying behaviors—physical and verbal telltale signs. I had to learn them in order to work as a research assistant in the psychology department. You exhibited, like, all of them. You're a terrible liar."

It was true, he'd been a textbook example. But I had no intention of ticking off *which* signs he'd shown. The ability to easily discern his truthfulness would be handy on an ongoing basis—or at least until we found Helena or figured out what had happened to her. I guess I shouldn't assume there'd be any ongoing anything after that.

He gave a sheepish, knowing laugh. "Helena always said I couldn't lie to save my life."

I waited a beat. "So, Mia Kim."

"Mia Kim was—is—Helena's therapist."

"Okay." That still didn't explain why he'd lied. I mean, at least half of New York City is in therapy. It's not some dark, shameful secret.

He cleared his throat. "She was pretty messed up when she got here from Rio. Being with Gabriel had done a real number on her self-esteem. She was depressed, thought she was worthless. I honestly believe Mia saved her life."

"Your sister was suicidal?" I asked gently.

He nodded wordlessly and hung his head.

I looked out the window at the lit-up skyline, jewels shining in the distance, and tried to think of something comforting to say. I wished Sage were here. She'd know the right words.

"I'm glad this Mia Kim person was able to help her," I finally offered.

He looked up at me. "Me too. But there's something else you should know." He reached inside his breast pocket and pulled out a square of paper that had been folded into fourths. He unfolded it, smoothed out the wrinkles, and handed it to me.

It was a note from Helena:

Dear Victor,

I'm sorry, but I can't do this anymore. He's never going to let me live in peace. There's no other way out.

I love you,

Helena

I read it a second time and then a third.

"What is this? Where did you get it?"

"It was on Helena's bedside table the first time we went to her apartment. You were preoccupied with that comforter, so I slipped it in my pocket before you could notice it."

"Why?"

"Why? Well, for one thing, it's addressed to me. But, more importantly, I didn't want you to see it and think it was a suicide note. Because that's not what it is."

"That's what it sounds like."

"I know that's what it sounds like," he said fiercely. "That's what it's supposed to sound like. So if Gabriel, or the police, or whoever found it, they'd think she went off somewhere to kill herself."

"But?" I prompted.

"But, if Helena were going to write a private note to me, a note like that, she'd have written it in Portuguese, not English."

"Probably," I conceded. "But she called her therapist. That suggests she was in crisis, doesn't it?"

"It could, but it could mean something else entirely. Read the note again," he directed.

I obliged. "Okay."

"What doesn't it say?"

"You mean what *does* it say?"

"No, I mean what I said. What doesn't it say?"

What was this? Some kind of Zen koan? I scanned the note again.

"I give up," I said.

"It *doesn't* say she's going to kill herself. You see? But that's where your mind went. And that's also the conclusion the police will immediately jump to—especially, if they know about Mia."

I reread the note. He was right.

"Okay, then what *do* you think she meant?"

He stood and started pacing as best he could in the tight space. "I think you may be right. I think she staged a fight scene with that fake blood and then took off."

"But why?"

"Because Gabriel found her. Or was about to, anyway, and she knew it. So she's gone into hiding. She probably called Mia for advice or support. And then she took off."

"Did she give you any clues in this note? Any hints at where she is?"

"None." A single word that weighed the world.

"Are you sure?"

He gave me a dark look. "I've read that damn note a hundred times, probably more. If there were a secret message, I'd have found it by now."

"Sorry." I felt bad pressing him, but if we were getting things out into the open, it was time for him to come clean about everything. I inhaled deeply and then hit him while he was down. "What about the box?"

"What box?"

"The first time we were in the apartment, you picked up a ring box from her bedside table and put it in your pocket."

He frowned. "That box was empty—trash. I was just getting rid of it."

I waited.

"It was the box her wedding ring came in. I recognized the jeweler's name. Gabriel's family always used that jewelry store."

"But the ring was gone?"

"The ring's *been* gone. She left it behind when she left Brazil. I know because I arranged for a friend to return it to Gabriel once she was safely out of the country. I don't understand why she left the box. It was right next the note, actually. I don't understand any of this. It's like a puzzle she thought I could solve. But I can't." He dragged his fingers through his hair. He was nearly vibrating with frustration.

"I'm sorry, Victor." I truly was. I came over to the bed and sat down next to him.

"It's not your fault."

I covered his hand with mine and squeezed. He squeezed back. We sat like that for a long time, listening to the blare of angry horns and faint sirens on the street below and the hushed ticking of the HVAC system in the walls.

Fourteen

Shortly before midnight, after liberating the minibar of a bottle of middling wine, a can of cashews, and couple of fair trade, dark chocolate bars (the combined cost of which probably would have covered a better-than-good dinner out), I had a brilliant thought. I sat bolt upright, dislodging his head from my shoulder.

"What's wrong?" His voice was sleepy, wine- and exhaustion-dulled.

"I have an idea!"

He rubbed his fists across his eyes. "Does it involve calling it a night and hitting the sheets?" He gestured toward the pitiful cot that housekeeping had delivered. It was still folded and propped against the wall. Anybody with enough spatial ability to park a car could look at it and tell there was no way it would fit in the available space if we opened it.

"No. Listen, I think I know how we can smoke out Gabriel. And maybe Helena, too."

His droopy eyelids flipped open. "Really?" he asked, suddenly alert.

"I think so. We think Helena vanished because she knew her ex-husband was getting close to finding her, right?"

"Right."

"And she left a fake suicide note."

"Right."

"But she also staged a struggle, which I don't get."

"You mean the fake blood?"

"Yeah." That bit was throwing me off. Had she staged a fight *and* her death at her own hands? It seemed like that should have been an either / or proposition, not both.

"I don't understand that part, either. Although, to be honest, I don't really understand any of this. Why didn't she just come to me for help?" His voice broke.

I tried to put myself in Helena's shoes. "She probably panicked. I don't know. But here's what I'm thinking. She wants Gabriel to think she's dead, right?"

"I think so."

"We need to have a funeral."

A look of pure horror crossed his face. "You're kidding."

"Okay, that sounded worse aloud than it did in my head. But hear me out. Given the fact that his goons are trailing us around town like baby ducks, he must not know where she is either and he's probably not sure she's even alive."

"Probably," he allowed.

He was still looking at me as if I'd sprouted devil's horns, but he hadn't run from the room screaming, so I figured I should push on.

"But if we visit a funeral home, a florist, go through the motions of planning a funeral, maybe it'll get back to him that she's dead."

"And what? He tucks his tail between his legs and goes back to Brazil?"

"No. Unless Lifetime Movies have lied to me, he'll show up at the funeral to see it with his own eyes. And that's when the police arrest him."

"You think the authorities are going to go along with this harebrained scheme? It's like something out of 'I Love Lucy.'"

"*Tom Sawyer*, actually, but whatever. And, yes, the police will play along because I'll ask a friend for a favor."

'Friends' may have been a slight overstatement of my actual relationship with Detective Dave Drummond, but I was confident he'd help me. Rosemary would see to it. Victor squinted, still unsure.

"It seems morbid."

"Morbid, but effective," I insisted.

"Maybe. You're forgetting the part where we sent Helena's phone on a tour of bars and breweries. Gabriel's guys are following a delivery truck now, not us."

I beamed at him. "Ah, if only we knew someone with an in at *The New York Times*. Tell me you know one of the obituary writers."

A spark of understanding lit his tired eyes. "This just might work."

"So what should we do first?"

"First, we sleep. I'll take the floor." He grabbed a pillow from the pile on the bed.

"Listen, we can share the bed. Just stay on your own side."

"Are you sure?"

"Sure. I mean, it's better than tripping over you and flying into a brick wall if I have to go to the bathroom in the middle of the night. This bed's plenty big for both of us. Just—"

"I know. Stay on my side." He gave me a meaningful look. "Trust me, Thyme, the first time I take you to bed for real, it won't be under these circumstances."

After dropping *that* bombshell, he brushed his teeth and fell asleep basically the second his head hit the pillow. I, on the other hand, lay awake staring at the ceiling, listening to his slow, even breathing and analyzing his last sentence a million different ways. Sometimes, a girl really needed to chat with her sisters.

~ ~ ~ ~ ~ ~ ~ ~ ~ ~

I came out of the steamy bathroom with a towel wrapped around my hair and a hotel bathrobe cinched tightly around my waist to find a room service tray and several bags from the boutique around the corner. Victor was munching on a cranberry muffin and wearing brand new dark gray trousers, a cream-colored dress shirt, and a black V-neck sweater.

"Morning," he said around a mouthful of pastry.

"Good morning. You look nice."

"We have a big day. I figured a fresh set of clothes was in order." He nodded toward the bags on the bed. "Hope I guessed your size correctly."

I peeked inside. A black wrap dress, an ivory cardigan, and a pair of impossibly high, scrappy black heels. I checked the tag on the dress. "The clothes should fit, but I'm not sure I'm going to be able to run from any attackers in those shoes."

He wrinkled his nose. "Good point."

"Tell you what, I'll just wear my ballet flats and hang onto these for that dinner at the Cuban restaurant you owe me."

A smile crossed his face. "It's a date." He brushed the crumbs from his fingers and gestured to the domed lid covering the tray. "You have a choice between oatmeal and a muffin. Orange juice and coffee. Eat up."

I helped myself to the oatmeal, swirling the dried fruit into it with my spoon. "So I figure our first order of business is to call my sister's boyfriend. Should we wait until it's a decent hour in California?"

"Do we have to?"

"Nah." I reached for my phone and reinserted the battery. While I waited for the phone to restart, I downed a cup of coffee then took my new outfit into the bathroom to get dressed. I dried my hair and piled it into a loose knot at the base of my neck. I added a swipe of matte red lipstick and some mascara and checked my reflection. I was a passable grieving friend.

I returned to the bedroom to call Rosemary and Dave. Victor was sitting on the bed with his notebook propped on his lap, chewing on the end of his pen.

"What are you doing?"

"Writing my sister's obituary," he answered without looking up.

I grabbed the phone and dialed Rosemary's number. She answered on the first ring.

"Are you alright?" Even though it wasn't yet seven o'clock on the West Coast, her voice was alert and anxious—and maybe a little bit irritated. "We've been worried sick about you ever since you sent that stupid text."

"I'm fine, Rosie. I'm sorry about the cryptic text, but I had a good reason."

"Right. Let me guess, traipsing around playing girl detective with a total stranger."

"Well, yeah. Listen, I really don't have time for the lecture right now. But I promise I'll call you later and let you harangue me for as long as you want."

"I'm not haranguing you," she harangued.

"Sure, okay. Lecture, scold, rant—you can pick the verb. But can we do it later, please?"

She was silent for a moment and then let out her breath in a big whoosh. "Fine. I'm sorry. I'm just worried."

"I know. I get it. I'm calling because I need your help." I knew that would get her attention. As the oldest, Rosemary *loved* to be consulted. She thrived on fixing problems for me and Sage, dispensing advice, and generally being in charge of our lives.

"Of course. Anything," she said instantly. "What's going on?"

I laid out the entire situation—the stage blood; the note addressed to Victor; the crazed gunmen stalking us; all of it. I paused for a breath.

"You spent the night with him?" she asked in a scandalized whisper.

"Focus, Rosemary. People were *shooting* at us."

"Right. Sorry. Okay, so what's the plan?"

"We need Dave to hook us up with someone he knows and trusts in local law enforcement. We think we can lure Helena's ex-husband into a trap, but we need someone to, you know, arrest him once we do."

"A trap?" Her voice dripped with skepticism.

"It'll work."

"Uh-huh."

"Can I please just talk to Dave?"

She huffed a little at that but passed the phone to her boyfriend.

"What's up, Thyme?"

I repeated the story for him, talking over his outburst when I got to the part about the Portuguese guys with the guns. I explained the fake funeral idea and then said, "Can you help us?"

He was silent for a long time—so long, in fact, that I thought our call might have gotten disconnected.

"Dave?"

"I'm here. I'm just speechless. I thought your sister here was the most reckless, idiotic woman alive when she tried to catch Amber's murderer singlehandedly."

"Dave—"

He rolled right over me. "But then, your *other* idiotic sister drove a flipping golf cart through a window to confront a murderer on that island in South Carolina, and I thought, no, Sage takes the cake."

"Listen—"

"But, now, now I see that this is hereditary. As a result of some genetic defect, the Field women seem to think they are superheroes with crime-fighting ability. Your plan is foolish, dangerous, and—"

"Let me stop you right there. First, I'll remind you that both Rosemary and Sage *succeeded*. Alayna's in prison for the murder of Amber Patrick and the attempted murder of her stepson. And Linda Zaharee is awaiting trial for her role in the murder of Fred Spears. So tell me again how stupid we are?"

"That's not a reason to risk your life," he sputtered.

"And, let's be clear, it's highly unlikely that this Gabriel dude has even ever killed anybody." That was a fairly weak argument, I realized. Not to mention that, for all I knew, he'd left behind a string of bodies that stretched across Rio de Janeiro. But I pressed on. "We're talking about two street punks and a dirty cop. That's all. Now are you going to help us or not?"

Dave sighed heavily. "I am. Not because your plan is so great, because, frankly, it sucks. And not because some guy you're hot for has conned you into playing amateur detective. And *not* because your crazy-ass sister is giving me the stink eye. I'm going to help you because there's nothing I hate more than a bent police office. Nothing." His voice was grim and resigned.

I flashed Victor a thumb's up sign.

"Thanks, Dave."

"Don't thank me. Grab a pen and write down this number."

Fifteen

It was a good thing we got an early start, because we had a million things to do. Victor didn't want to ask his buddy with the car service business for another favor, what with the whole 'sorry, we returned your car with a shattered rear window and a body riddled with bullet holes' thing. But we also couldn't burn the entire day riding around on the subway. So we flagged down a cab and headed to a bone broth shop in the East Village to meet Dave's friend, an officer assigned to the NYPD's Movie/Television Unit. Yes, that's really a thing—they're both a thing, actually. The broth takeout place and the Movie/TV unit.

Patrol officer Jerry Thompson met us outside the broth joint. He was already standing on line, wearing his crisp blue uniform and a pair of aviator glasses. He waved me over. Victor paid the driver.

"Officer Thompson?"

He pushed the sunglasses up to the top of his head and flashed me a dazzlingly white smile. It rivaled Victor's for brightness. What was the story with these New York men and their pearly whites?

"Ms. Field."

His handshake was firm but not bone-crushing. Victor joined us.

"This is the friend I mentioned on the phone. Victor Callais, Officer Thompson." I made the introductions while the two men sized one another up and shook hands.

"Thanks for meeting us," Victor said.

"No problem. Thanks for coming out here. I'm assigned to a shoot around the corner."

We inched up in the line of people waiting to drop actual hard-earned cash on a cup of broth.

"Has anyone ever told you that you look exactly like Ryan Samson?" I tried hard to stop myself from actually saying the words, but it was impossible. He looked *just like* the movie star. In fact, for a moment I wondered if maybe he actually *was* Ryan Samson, doing some sort of Method acting preparation for a role as a police officer.

He threw back his head and laughed. "I may have heard that once or twice." He leaned in conspiratorially. "I actually appeared in *Blue Blood, Big Badge* as his stunt double in a scene."

"Really?" Beside me, I felt Victor stiffening with impatience and boredom. "I mean, is that part of your job?"

Victor snorted, but Officer Thompson nodded. "Sort of. The Movie and Television Unit provides traffic control to productions being filmed in the city. We also oversee 'crime scenes' for shows like *CSI* and *Law and Order*. Think about it. It would be pretty horrifying for a citizen to wander into a scene where the actors have found a murdered body. We keep them back, just as we would from a real crime scene. And officers from the unit appear in crowd scenes where police officers are needed. We aren't paid extra for that," he hurried to explain. "It's part of the job. But it's better than having a bunch of folks running around the boroughs impersonating police officers, you know?"

In a crazy way, it made sense. It blurred the lines between fact and fiction, life and entertainment, but the existence of the unit and the role they filled probably did keep New Yorkers safer than they otherwise would be. And, no doubt, helped boost the economy by bringing movie crews and television shows to town.

"I see," Victor intoned, having no doubt undertaken the same silent analysis.

Officer Thompson went on. "As for Ryan Samson, I actually have my SAG card because when he needed someone to be his body double, that was outside the scope of my role with the unit. I was a paid actor in that scene." He puffed out his chest.

"Wow, what did you do?" I hadn't actually seen *Blue Blood, Big Badge*, but I remembered the trailers. "Were you in the rooftop shoot out?"

"No, not that scene."

"Were you hanging from the window washer lift, fighting the bad guys in the Empire State Building scene?" Victor asked.

"Um, no not that one either." His chest deflated and his shoulders sagged. "It was the scene where he was racing to catch the L Train. He didn't want to go down into the station. I guess he's afraid of rats."

I flashed back to the furry rodent that had scampered across my legs under the table in that Chinese restaurant and shuddered.

"That was a good scene, too," Victor mumbled.

After an awkward pause, the patrolman cleared his throat. "How do you know Dave Drummond?"

The line snaked forward and we inched along with it, moving incrementally closer to the takeout window.

"My oldest sister is dating him. They met when he was investigating Amber Patrick's death. She was Amber's private chef." I tried to explained the knotty, tangled situation as simply as possible.

His eyes sparked—whether at the mention of the late rom-com superstar or the scandalous murder that had captivated the tabloids, I couldn't tell. But he simply said, "Gotcha."

"How do you know Dave?"

"The LAPD was considering reorganizing to form a unit like ours. Some of us flew out there to give them a presentation; then a couple months later, a couple of their guys, including Dave, came here to see us in action. We both like opera. We caught a showing of *Sweeney Todd* when it was in town."

The fact that Detective Dave was an opera buff was news to me. I filed that piece of information for later use, like if I got his name in a family gift exchange. We reached the window. Officer Thompson ordered a medium cup of broth and handed over a ten-dollar bill.

He turned toward us, clutching his steaming take-out cup in his hands. "Aren't you going to get something? Try the beef," he suggested.

"We already had breakfast," I demurred. I was well-acquainted with the nutritional benefits of stock made from the roasted bones. My mother had been a big believer. As a result, I was also well-acquainted with how easily (and inexpensively) I could make an enormous vat of the stuff at home. I might pay five bucks for an overpriced chai latte, but dropping a ten on broth? I was *far* too frugal for that nonsense.

"Suit yourself." He took a big swig from his cup and exhaled contentedly. "So what can I do for you two?"

We started walking away from the broth shop and, presumably, toward the cordoned-off area where the movie crew was shooting.

"Victor's sister is missing," I began.

"She an adult?" he asked between sips.

Victor nodded. "She's twenty-five."

"You file a missing person's report yet?"

"No, see—"

The officer cut him off. "Don't believe what you see on television. Ha. That probably sounds funny coming from me, but it's true. You should definitely report her missing. It's not the waste of time those shows make it out to be."

"That's not why I didn't call the police," Victor explained. He took a long breath before plunging into his story. "Helena, my sister, was married to a dirty cop—er, police officer—back home in Brazil. He abused her. She got away from him. I helped her get settled here and she filed for divorce. But she's always been worried that he'd find her."

Officer Thompson paused with his cup mid-air and gave a sad *tsk*. "That's rough, man. I'm sorry."

"Yeah. Gabriel, her ex, he's connected. He worked on a high-profile cross-border drug case with the federal DEA and some guys from NYPD Narcotics. I ... I'm not sure who to trust."

Thompson's entire face stiffened into a cement mask as he bristled at the notion that New York's finest might not all be on the up and up. After a moment, though, he relaxed his jaw. "There's bad apples everywhere," he acknowledged. "But if that's how you feel, why are we talking now?"

I piped up. "We've been looking for her ourselves, but we're not making a ton of progress. And ... there are two guys following us around, um, trying to kill us."

His eyebrows jumped up his smooth forehead. "Did you say *kill* you?"

"They took a couple shots at us near Hell's Kitchen yesterday. Luckily, they have crappy aim," I explained.

He closed his eyes and muttered something unintelligible under his breath. Then he exhaled, flaring his nostrils, and looked straight at me. "So what do you want to do about it?"

"We want to stage a funeral. That's where you come in."

Sixteen

atrol Officer Jerry Thompson was a man of action. I had barely finished explaining the plan when he chugged the rest of his beef broth and radioed for assistance, barking out commands in an alphabet soup of abbreviations that meant nothing to me. Victor pulled out his cell phone and called in Helena's obituary. I could tell from his face that he felt guilty about misleading a coworker, but he plowed forward anyway. That just left me.

I squared my shoulders and fixed my resolve. *You can do this, Thyme. She puts her bra on backwards and then wriggles it around after it's been fastened, just like everyone else.*

I punched in the numbers and threw in a soft *ohm* mantra while I waited to be connected.

Maura's chipper voice sounded in my ear. "Whittier Media, Cate Whittier-Clay's office. How may I help you?"

"Maura, it's Thyme Field. I need to see Cate."

"You need to see her? Like, you need to reschedule her workout or you want to make an appointment with her?"

"More like, I'm on my way with a reporter from the *Times* and an NYPD officer."

Maura gasped. I smiled to myself. The statement was one hundred percent true, but I knew that Maura would misinterpret it the way I'd intended and think something was going down that involved Whittier Media. I heard the clatter of keys as she shuffled around appointments to clear a hole in Cate's always-crammed schedule.

"Um, it looks like she has an opening at eleven. Can you be here that soon?"

I glanced at my watch. It would be tight, but presumably Officer Movie Star had lights and a siren.

"We'll be there. Thanks, Maura."

She dropped her voice to a whisper. "Sage, do I need to call Cate's attorney?"

I decided to take pity on her—in no small part because Cate was going to freak out on her for giving us an appointment no matter what; I might as well try to mitigate the damage.

"No, that's not necessary at this point. Just tell Cate that Whittier Media isn't implicated in this, um, police business. But let her know her help will be instrumental *and* will generate lots of good will from law enforcement and, more importantly, good press from *The New York Times*."

Victor caught my eye and quirked his mouth as if to say 'Oh, really?' I just smiled. For all Cate's rah-rah new media cheerleading, she still craved legitimacy. And in her eyes, it didn't get any more legit than the paper of record.

On the other end of the phone, Maura let out a happy sigh. "I can definitely sell that," she said, relief and enthusiasm replacing the dread in her voice. "See you in a few."

I ended the call and joined Victor and Officer Thompson, who were standing near a black-and-white patrol car. Officer Thompson was gesturing a lot and talking in a loud, animated voice to an unimpressed female officer.

"No. *Nein. Nyet.* Am I speaking your language yet?" she asked.

"Come on, Jennings. Just lend me your wheels." He flashed that movie star grin at her.

Jennings appeared to be immune to his stunt double charms. She shook her head and crossed her arms over her chest. "I'm not hoofing it back to the station after this shoot. I drove, you lose."

He craned his neck and looked at Victor. "Okay if Jennings tags along? She's a straight shooter."

Victor glanced at me. I didn't like it. You know the saying, three can keep a secret if two of them are dead? Four seemed even worse. But we had to get to Cate's office before we got bumped from our slot. Maura was a lot of things, but she wasn't a magician. She couldn't hold Cate's schedule open indefinitely.

I forced a smile. "Sure."

Officer Jennings eyed us for a moment with a neutral look and then turned and shouted to another patrol officer, "Jerry and I have to talk to a wit in midtown. Hold down the fort."

The guy gave a two-fingered salute and went back to chatting up the makeup artist.

Officer Thompson ushered us into the back of the car then he and Jennings engaged in what appeared to be ritual bickering over the best route to the Whittier Media Building. Only after she acquiesced to following his directions, did we finally pull out into the flow of traffic. It occurred to me that the workplace dynamics between colleagues in a high-stress environment like law enforcement would make for fertile research ground.

Then I laughed at myself. *As if.* The odds of my returning to my graduate program grew longer by the day. I figured Cate was more likely than not to fire me for canceling her workout. And if she did can me, I wouldn't be able to pay my share of the balloon payment on my parents' debt. And we'd lose the resort.

Stop it, I told myself as Jennings hit the lights, activated the siren, and zoomed through an intersection, honking, shouting, and cursing at the drivers who were moving aside too slowly for her liking. *All this worst-case bellyaching isn't going to help. Worry doesn't change anything.* It was one of my father's favorite sayings, only he put a dopey dad spin on it: *Don't borrow sorrow from tomorrow.*

Victor gave me a concerned look, almost as if he could hear my thoughts, and squeezed my hand in his. Officer Thompson twisted around to talk to us through the wire cage that separated the back seat from the front.

"I called back to the squad room to get some more bodies on this. I figure we'll need at least three or four blues in addition to me and Jennings here."

I opened my mouth to protest, but Victor beat me to it. "I think we need to be very discreet, given the ... connections I mentioned before."

Thompson waved a hand at his concerns. "Listen, don't worry about that. Your guy's some kind of undercover narcotics agent, right?"

"Yes." Victor stared meaningfully at the back of Officer Jennings head.

"Right. We're pulling together a team from Movie and TV. There's two kinds of officers in my unit. Guys—"

"And gals," Jennings corrected him.

"Guys *and gals* who were assigned by the luck of the draw, and guys and gals who came to the Big Apple with stars in their eyes. You know? Like, they moved here, waited tables and acted in crappy theater productions for a couple years and then realized their dreams were childish and unrealistic and joined the force. But, in their hearts, they think, maybe, just maybe, this is their chance to be discovered." His voice grew distant, and his eyes were looking at something far off.

"You're in the latter group, aren't you?" I asked quietly.

He nodded. "It's true. But the point is nobody goes from narcotics to Movie and TV. Just doesn't happen that way. Your skell isn't gonna have a contact in my unit. We're on solid ground." He sounded so certain that I felt my shoulders unknotting.

"If you're sure."

"I'm positive." He turned back to the front and resumed poking at his partner's driving skills.

I don't know what kind of magic Maura worked on Cate, but she was barely fuming at all by the time we were ushered into her massive office, all white leather, hard angles, and glass. She looked at us over the top of her reading glasses when we traipsed into the room then waved her hand toward the sitting area, which consisted of two white couches facing one another across a Lucite and steel coffee table.

As she crossed the room to join us, Maura rattled off introductions and then stood at attention just inside the door, waiting to be dismissed. I'd already explained in the car that Cate did not shake hands. Germs, you know. So no one made the mistake of advancing toward our hostess with an outstretched hand.

"Thank you, Maura. Why don't you order up some coffee for our guests. Does anyone prefer tea?"

"Green tea would be great," Officer Thompson said.

Maura nodded and then backed out of the room. The two police officers stood awkwardly in front of the couch to the left of the table. Victor and I took seats on the one to the right. Cate started to lower herself into the captain's chair at the end of the coffee table and stopped, hovering with her butt just inches above the cushion, waiting for Officers Thompson and Jennings to sit down first. They continued to stand there stiffly.

Finally, Cate sat down and crossed her legs. Only then did the two officers take seats on the couch. I had a feeling that the delay was the result, not of some etiquette rule regarding sitting with civilians, but of a prearranged effort to throw the high-powered executive off kilter. Judging by the squat Cate had just performed, it seemed to have worked.

"Maura tells me you need my help," Cate said without preamble, directing her question to the police officers. She removed her glasses and twirled them around by one of the stems while she waited for an answer.

"Yes, ma'am," Jennings confirmed, even though she hadn't exactly been filled in on the details of what we were doing in Cate's office.

Officer Thompson cleared his throat. "Our department, the Movie and Television Unit, is coordinating with Mr. Callais here on a sting operation." He gestured toward Victor.

Cate turned her head in our direction. "And you're a reporter from *The New York Times*."

It was a statement, not a question, but Victor answered it anyway. "That's correct."

Her cool blue eyes slid over my face and she gave me a look that said, 'I'll deal with you and your bout of fake food poisoning later.' Then she fixed her icy gaze back on Victor. "Now what would a financial reporter be doing in the middle of a Movie and Television matter?"

One point for Cate (well, Maura). She'd done some research before we arrived. Although, minus one point because she didn't seem to connect the surname Callais to her missing nanny. So, net gain: zero points.

"Actually, it's more that the authorities are helping me with a private matter," he told her in a professorial tone.

"Oh?"

She waited.

"My sister is missing. We have reason to believe she's hiding from her abusive ex-husband, who just happens to be in law enforcement."

"Oh, I'm so sorry to hear that," Cate said in a voice that sounded more bored than sympathetic. "But I'm not sure how any of this involves Whittier Media."

"My sister is Helena Callais. Your nanny." His voice cracked. I patted his thigh in a quick gesture and hoped no one noticed.

"Ah. The vanishing Helena. You know, Audra's still crying herself to sleep."

He grimaced. "I'm sorry to hear that. And I know that Helena would be, too. She's very fond of your daughter." He leaned forward and braced his elbows on his knees. "You have to believe me—if she didn't believe her life was in danger, she never would have pulled a disappearing act."

At the words 'her life was in danger,' Cate suddenly became interested in the conversation. She sat up straight and gave Victor her full attention.

"I've been trying to find her—with Thyme's help," he continued.

"Thyme's a yoga instructor," Cate pointed out.

"Yogalates, actually."

They both ignored me. Victor said, "She has a background in psychology and has been instrumental in helping me try to figure out what happened to Helena."

Cate pursed her lips and appraised me for a moment as if maybe I wasn't *quite* as limited as she'd always believed.

"And what did you two learn?"

"We learned that Gabriel, Helena's ex, had been in contact with her. We learned that she staged a violent scene at her apartment before she took off, and we learned that Gabriel has at least two armed, dangerous men combing the streets of New York looking for her."

"That's where you come in," Officer Thompson interjected. He lowered his voice an octave or two, maybe in an effort to sound more official. Whatever the reason, it seemed to work.

"Of course. What can I do to help?"

A small knock sounded on the door. I walked over and opened it for Maura, who wheeled in a cart of drinks and snacks.

"Thanks," she whispered. And then she was gone as quickly as she'd come. I wondered whether she had a stomach ulcer. I wondered how much money she made as the assistant to an uptight, controlling media mogul and whether it was worth all the stress.

My musings were interrupted by the realization that everyone was looking at me.

"Sorry, what did I miss?" I asked, flustered.

"It's your plan, Thyme. You should do the honors," Victor said.

"Oh, uh, okay." I returned my coffee mug to the cart and kept my hands steady by sheer force of will. Cate Whittier-Clay made me nervous when she was in a modified camel's pose with her elbows pinned behind her back and her face red from concentration and her consistent failure to *breathe* while she exercised. Sitting in her corner office, wearing her stylish Nina McLemore suit, and staring at me with rapt attention, she absolutely terrified me. She may as well have been breathing actual fire.

"Based on everything we know, Helena went underground because she knew Gabriel was coming for her. And, given the way his thugs are acting, she made the right call. But, she didn't leave any way for anyone to contact her—probably an effort to protect her family and her friends—and *your* family. So I was thinking if we had a high-profile, well-publicized funeral for her, then it might achieve two goals: one, it will probably smoke out Gabriel—or at least his henchmen. And they'll give him up, right?" I turned to the police officers.

"They always do on television," Officer Thompson deadpanned.

"And the second goal?" Cate asked.

"If it gets enough press, Helena might find out about it. Since she knows she's not dead, maybe she'll reach out to Victor—or one of her friends." That second part seemed weaker in the cold light of Cate's office than it had at midnight through a haze of exhaustion and wine, but I nodded with authority as I said it.

Cate blinked. "Don't take this the wrong way—but are we sure she's alive?"

I hesitated, thinking about the note in Victor's pocket.

"No," he said in a thick, strangled voice. "We're not."

The air suddenly felt heavy and hot. The only sound in the otherwise silent room was the noise of Officer Jennings chewing as she gnawed her way through a handful of Cate's favorite chef-made granola.

"Sorry," she said around a mouthful. "This stuff's addictive."

Officer Thompson threw her a dark look. "It's possible Ms. Callais is dead," he said with all the finesse you'd imagine. "But it's worth a shot to see if we can get this Vasquez dirtbag off the streets. So what we need you to do is to go on your channel and do a ... what's it called?"

"A Cate the Great segment about losing your nanny in a tragic fashion," I supplied. Cate did these periodic essays as if she were Mickey Rooney's spiritual heir. They focused on her challenges as a working mother and a female CEO. Because nothing speaks more to the plight of the working woman than a multimillionaire with a staff of a half-dozen and money to throw at all her problems. But apparently, her audience loved them. She aired them on-line on her Periscope channel and plastered them all over social media. Inevitably, they went viral, aided—of course—by the pieces her columnists wrote about them and the mentions they got from cable show talking heads.

She tilted her head in thought. "Hmm. It would certainly resonate. But it's fundamentally dishonest. Whittier Media prides itself on its authenticity. I simply don't elevate anything above the truth—not entertainment, not information, and, I'm afraid, not even helping the authorities."

I stared at Officer Thompson. He gave me a blank look. I thought that was it, but Officer Jennings saved our bacon.

"Absolutely. I'm a big fan, Ms. Whittier-Clay, and I would *never* expect anything less from you. But I don't think Ms. Field and Mr. Callais are planning to ask you to lie. And certainly, the NYPD wouldn't agree to be part of something that's not aboveboard. We've put in a permit for a live theatrical performance at Our Lady of Pompeii—that's a Roman Catholic Church located in the Village. It's where Ms. Callais worshipped. The play, if you will, will feature amateur actors, including Mr. Callais and Ms. Field, as well as several members of the Movie / TV Unit, who will be strategically placed around the venue. And you and your family, if you'd like to participate. We'll work with you to craft a public statement that doesn't contain any blatant lies."

Cate shook her head slightly. "How ... politic."

Officer Thompson leaned forward. "It's for the greater good."

"And *The Times* is going along with this?" she addressed Victor.

He made a face like he had indigestion. It was true that the newspaper was running Helena's obituary. But his employer didn't necessarily know it was a ruse. Finally, he settled for the partial truth. "Yes."

She puffed out her cheeks and exhaled. "I don't like it. But I want to help your sister; Audra just adores her. And I have my own reasons. My mother was a victim of domestic abuse."

The room fell silent once more. This time, even Officer Jennings paused in her chewing. Cate got a faraway look in her eyes and said, "Well, let's get this thing written and get on with it."

Seventeen

From Cate's office I headed straight home, tailed by the junior patrolman that Officer Thompson had insisted on assigning to protect me. The officer escorted me to my apartment and then returned to the street, where he sat in a squad car positioned so he could see the front door to my building and my window.

Victor had also been sent home with his designated bodyguard. After all the tension and activity, I felt oddly lonely and at loose ends alone in my apartment. If I'm being honest, I also missed his company.

I ate a light dinner, did a long stretching routine, then wandered around for a while, pacing aimlessly in the small space. Finally I drew a bath, adding calming essential oils to the hot water. I took a mug of herbal tea and my cellphone into the bathroom with me. I slipped into the tub and conference called my sisters.

"Are you okay?"

"It's about time!"

They started talking over one another immediately. The combination of mother henning, scolding, and concern should have raised my already-high anxiety level through the ceiling, but I found it oddly comforting. More so than the bath and tea, even. My sisters' attention and fretting was like an old, soft robe—familiar and cozy. It felt like love. I sunk further into the water and closed my eyes.

"I'm fine. I'm safe and sound with a police officer posted down on the street in front of my building," I assured them.

"And Victor?" Sage asks in this sly, wink-wink-nudge-nudge voice.

"He's right here in the bath with me," I said dryly. "Also safe and sound."

Predictably, Rosemary gave a scandalized gasp, and Sage giggled. I felt my lips curve into a smile.

"Kidding, Rosie. I'm just joking. He's back at his place—also with a uniformed babysitter."

"Thyme, really. So I take it Dave's contact was able to help you?"

"He was. Officer Thompson is an interesting guy. He could pass for Ryan Samson's twin ...." I paused to wait for Sage's dreamy sigh. She *claimed* her new boyfriend Roman bore more than a passing resemblance to the movie star, as well. But seeing as how the guy was wearing a golf cap and sunglasses in just about every picture she sent us, who could know?

I continued. "He and his partner helped us convince Cate to post one of her video chats. It should be live now. Hang on; I'll send it."

I dried my free hand on the towel I'd had the foresight to hang over the edge of the bathtub then navigated to Cate's Periscope channel. I forwarded the link to my sisters so we could watch it together. Although at this point, Maura had no doubt already saved and shared it to Instagram, Facebook, Twitter, and a whole slew of other social media sites I was way too unhip to even know existed.

"Got it," Rosemary said.

"Me, too," Sage chimed in.

I hit the replay and watched as Cate leaned forward and stared into the camera with a sad smile and eyes that promised to fill with tears at any moment. She blinked and started speaking:

"Hi, friends. You know I like to keep my Cate the Great segments upbeat and inspiring. I usually focus on all the GREAT parts of being a working mama. But today's a sad day for this mom ... and for her little girl. I'm sure I've mentioned Audra's beloved nanny before. Helena's been caring for my sweetpea since I returned to work full-time; although, of course, I worked very hard even before I came back to the office. Remember what I always say: balance is a myth; aim to stretch!

Anyway, New York's Finest paid me a visit today." She paused here and choked back what sounded like real tears. "Helena went missing last weekend. I scrambled to arrange a patchwork of care for little Audra, always believing that it would be a temporary solution. Today, I learned it's permanent. Tomorrow, I'll have to take my sweet angel to Our Lady of Pompeii Shrine Church at eleven a.m. to say goodbye to **her** *sweet angel, Helena Callais. Our Lady of Pompeii is the Roman Catholic Church in Greenwich Village that welcomes immigrants, those who speak Portuguese, in particular. It makes sense that Helena, who was from Brazil, would want to have her funeral Vigil held at Our Lady. I hope you'll take a moment to think of us tomorrow and to give your pumpkin an extra squeeze before you leave for work. Cate Out."*

Rosemary spoke first. "Nice plug for her 'Strength, Not Balance' Campaign."

I snorted. "It wasn't nearly as clunky as the part where she explained where the Vigil would be, and why. But hey, if you parse her words, she didn't actually say anything that's demonstrably false. She's pretty good."

"If by good, you mean slippery and disingenuous, I agree."

I let Sage's disapproval go unchallenged. She worked for a stay-at-home socialite. Muffy Moore and Cate Whittier-Clay were as different as two mothers could be. Sage agreed with Muffy's parenting style, for the most part. So it stood to reason she found Cate's lacking.

"As long as it works," I said.

"And if it does work, what then?"

"The hope is that both Gabriel and Helena hear about Helena's funeral and can't resist showing up. Ideally, not at the same time."

"And then?" Rosemary pressed.

"Then the police arrest Gabriel and his minions, and Helena lives happily ever after."

"Don't you mean Victor and Thyme live happily ever after?" Sage asked.

I thought about that for a moment. "I'm not sure. Circumstances threw us together. This might just be an adrenaline-fueled fling, not a serious thing."

They both started hooting and laughing at me.

I pulled the phone away from my ear and huffed in irritation. "What's so funny?"

"You are," Sage gasped between laughs. "Rosemary met Dave while he was investigating her for murder. And I rescued Roman from a killer. But, yeah, nobody starts a committed relationship under those sort of conditions."

"You're so clueless, little sis. But that's why we love you." Rosemary's amusement was tinged with affection.

"Whatever. I have to go. I need to get a good night's sleep for my big day."

We ended the call and I traded my phone for my mug of tea. I focused on relaxing my muscles and then my mind. I was so chill I didn't hear the *ping* that announced the arrival of a text message.

It wasn't until I drained the bath and wrapped myself in my robe that I glanced at the screen and saw the notification. The text was from Victor.

Cate's going viral. NYT obit in the a.m. Pieces all in place. Only thing missing is you beside me.

Warm anticipation blossomed in my chest and a stupid grin bloomed on my lips. I went to bed laughing at the giddy schoolgirl feelings that the financial reporter from Brazil stirred in me.

Sweet dreams, I texted back before I turned out the lights.

Eighteen

I slept soundly and was awake well before the sun. But it felt strange to be back to my ordinary routine, even though I'd deviated from it for one day. It was as if the time I'd spent dodging gun-wielding attackers with Victor had changed everything—separating my life neatly into *Before Victor* and *After Victor* eras. Or maybe *Before Bad Guys* and *After Bad Guys*. Either way, I had to force myself to stay present in the moment as I met with my early morning clients.

During Cate Whittier-Clay's workout, she focused entirely on her flexibility exercises and didn't so much as mention the upcoming sham funeral vigil or the buzz surrounding her viral video. It was as though the visit to her office the day before had never happened. For once, I appreciated her laser-like attention on herself.

After Cate's session, as I was leaving the Whittier-Clay penthouse, Audra peeked out from her bedroom.

"Thyme?" she said in a small voice, her face half hidden by the door.

"Good morning, Audra."

"Helena's in heaven with Nana Clay, now. Did you know that?" Her little lips wobbled but she didn't cry.

My heart sank. I'd hoped Cate would have kept the 'news' about Helena from her daughter. I walked over to the door and crouched to address her at her eye level.

"I know you cared a lot about Helena. And I know she cared a lot about you." I didn't know what else to say.

Luckily I didn't have to try to come up with something, because just then Janie appeared in the doorway behind Audra. She held a black silk ribbon in one hand and a hairbrush in the other.

"Come on, sweetness, it's time to do your hair and put on your dress."

"But I don't want to wear black. Yellow was Helena's favorite color, like the sun." Her lower lip started trembling again. This time, tears fell from her eyes, too. Fat, fast tears that ran down her cheeks in rivulets.

Janie put down the brush and hair bow and picked up the little girl. Audra threw her arms around her new nanny's neck. Janie rubbed her back and made a soothing, repetitive hushing sound. I took a step closer and caught the other woman's eye.

"Cate's not really planning to take her to the church, is she?"

Janie raised her eyebrows and gave me a look that said it all. "Mr. Clay and I shared our thoughts about the idea, but Ms. Whittier-Clay feels that it's important that the press see that she treats her daughter like a little human being and allows her to mourn."

I bit down so hard that I drew blood from my lower lip. *Un-freaking-believable. Cate not only told her kid that her beloved nanny was dead, she was going to drag the poor thing to the fake funeral vigil because of the optics. Nice.*

Once I thought I could speak without shrieking, I said, "At least let her wear yellow."

The nanny held my gaze for a long moment. "I suppose it would be fine. Poor girl. So much heartache for a little one." She continued to rub Audra's narrow back. The girl rested her head on Janie's shoulder and sighed.

I backed out of the room and reversed course, headed not to the front door but to Cate's kitchen, where I found her sipping her smoothie, her wet hair wrapped in a towel. She looked up from the newspaper, which was spread out on the massive marble island.

"Did you forget something?"

"No. I need to talk to you."

She arched an eyebrow but turned to her chef, who was busily cleaning the Vitamix blender. "Martin, leave that. I need to speak to Thyme for a moment."

He turned off the water and bobbed his head then scurried away from the sink and out of the kitchen.

She waited a beat. "Well?"

"Well, I don't think you should have told Audra that Helena's dead."

"That's none of your business." She took a sip of frothy green liquid and eyed me over the glass.

"That's true," I conceded. "But she's in her room crying her eyes out over something you know isn't true."

"Oh, this is rich. *You're* lecturing *me* about honesty? You seem to have an exceedingly casual relationship with the truth, Thyme. Here I am reading a fabricated death notice." She slapped her hand down on the newspaper. "And you lied about being sick to get out of our session yesterday; you concocted this entire falsehood about Helena's death and *begged* me to play along. And now you're going to take me to task about doing just that?"

My cheeks burned because she was one hundred percent correct. I nodded. "I deserve that. But Audra doesn't deserve this misery, Ca—Ms. Whittier-Clay. She's just a child."

"I know she's a child. She's *my* child. And as a result, the press will expect her to be at the vigil. I can't very well take her without letting her know what it's about. So, you have only yourself to blame for any sadness she's feeling."

I stared at her for a long moment wondering if she actually had a heart or if maybe she was some sort of ultrarealistic-looking android. I decided to try another tack.

"It won't be safe. If the plan works, we'll be luring a violent, vengeful man into the church. You can't bring a three-year-old into—"

She raised a palm. "Let me stop you right there. I can see you don't think much of my mothering but I've already communicated the safety issue to Officer Thompson. He's added two additional officers to the crew. They'll be masquerading as caterers, so they'll be in the basement kitchen the entire time. As soon as the officers positioned on the street send word that Gabriel Vasquez has been spotted, my family will be whisked down to the basement and protected by the men there. So spare me your concern."

I thought she was done, so I turned to leave. She drained her glass and put it down on the island just a bit harder than was necessary.

"Oh, and Thyme?"

I faced her. "Yes?"

"What you should be concerning yourself with is whether you'll be losing a client as a result of your dishonesty. I don't think you fully comprehend how valuable my time is. You wasted it yesterday morning; that's not something I'm going to forgive lightly."

My stomach churned. Cate was my most lucrative client. She paid a premium to have her session at her convenience, and she demanded a high degree of attention. I knew I was supposed to grovel now. But I couldn't do it. I had to live with myself, after all.

I squared my shoulders. "If you think you can find another instructor with my level of experience, feel free. But I won't apologize for prioritizing the safety of another human being over your ability to execute a full split. And, if, as you say, you have past experience with domestic violence, I can't imagine you'd expect me to."

I held myself ramrod straight and hurried out of the penthouse without waiting to see her reaction. I made it all the way to the elevator before I gave into my shaking knees and leaned against the wall.

~ ~ ~ ~ ~ ~ ~ ~ ~ ~

I was still more than a bit jittery when I raced home to change out of my yoga clothes and into something more appropriate for church. I hated confrontation more than anyone I knew, and standing up to Cate Whittier-Clay was something I never dreamed I'd do.

When I'd come out of Cate's building, Officer Leah Yee, who'd relieved the poor guy who'd sat outside my building overnight, bolted out of her squad car and grabbed my elbow. She said I looked so pale that she was afraid I was going to faint and had insisted on stopping at a corner market to get me a bottled water on our way to my apartment.

My heart rate had returned to normal during the drive, but my hands were still clammy and the tight knot in my stomach showed no signs of dissipating. If Cate fired me, I really would have to scramble to make up the lost income.

Don't borrow sorrow from tomorrow, Thyme, I reminded myself for the second time in as many days. Thinking about my dad just made me think about what he and my mother had done. My whirring thoughts were going from bad to worse now.

I needed to still my mind before it spun completely out of control. I didn't really have time for it, but I needed it. I settled myself on a thin cushion on the floor of my studio, crossed my legs in lotus position, rested my palms on my thighs, and fixed my gaze on the floorboard about four inches away. I let my thoughts pass without focusing on them.

When my breathing was even and my stomach was unknotted, I exhaled one final time and then unfolded my legs and stood. I checked the time and strode purposefully toward my bathroom shower stall where I'd hung the black dress that Victor had given me while I'd showered earlier. That was one of my mom's tricks. Back in the days before green dry cleaning (whatever that was), she'd been leery of the chemicals used by our neighborhood cleaner. So she always hung her dressy clothes in the bathroom to give them a good steam while she showered.

I hoped nobody would notice when I showed up in the same dress I'd worn yesterday, but I didn't have a lot of choices. Most of my clothes were appropriate for the exercise studio, a girls' night out on the town, or cleaning my apartment. Aside from the black dress, the only thing I owned that was even remotely appropriate was a navy and white chevron print maxidress—and that was a real stretch. Not to mention, I sort of wanted to save that for the date that Victor had promised.

A small thrill of excitement ran through me at the thought, and I rolled my eyes at myself.

Ten minutes later, I met Officer Yee on the sidewalk in front of my building, looking entirely presentable, if I do say so myself.

"Feeling better?" She asked.

"I am."

She nodded. "You look better." Then she glanced down at my feet and gave a nod of approval. "Flats. Smart—in case you need to run."

In case I need to run?

After she ushered me into the car and entered the flow of traffic, I leaned forward and asked, "Do you like working in the Movie and Television Unit?" It was my lame attempt at small talk in the hopes that chatting would distract me from the images of scenes I might need to run from today.

"Oh, no, I'm not assigned to Movie and TV."

"What?" I was sure I'd misheard her.

The hint of panic in my voice must have registered because her eyes slid up to the rearview mirror and met mine. "Don't worry, Ms. Field. You're in good hands. I've been in the Patrol Services Bureau for six years. I've got your back."

"Oh, sure, of course. I'm just surprised. Officer Thompson and Officer Jennings said this, um, play would be staffed entirely by officers from the Movie and Television Unit. It's ... well, it's a groundbreaking performance," I finished lamely because I had no idea how much, if anything, Officer Yee knew about what we actually planned to do at Our Lady of Pompeii. But given her cryptic comment about running, I figured she knew *something*.

"No sweat. I'm just your ride. I'm supposed to hand you over to Jennings and Thompson at the church and then go back to patrol duty. I guess the Mayor's Office of Media and Entertainment was chapped that Thompson got so many bodies assigned to your, uh, *play*. Somebody from over there called up the Planning Of-

ficer and ripped him a new one because a movie star-
ring His Honor's favorite actress got shafted on traffic
control. They had to do a lot of last minute shuffling
and ring kissing to make everyone happy." She shared
the news about the interdepartmental squabble almost
gleefully, as if the sheer pettiness of the problem delighted her.

It occurred to me that it likely *did* delight her. She
probably saw more than her share of humanity's dark
underbelly. A pissing contest that started because the
mayor had a crush on some movie star? Now that was
likely nothing but entertainment for Officer Yee.

But, for me, it was another thing to worry about.
The team Officer Thompson had assembled was being
reshuffled. Cate was bringing her three-year old. And
that blasted knot was back in the pit of my stomach.

Nineteen

Officer Yee sat in her patrol car right at the corner of Carmine and Bleeker Street, idling and watching, waiting for me to go ahead and pull open the giant wood doors that led into the massive, block-long church. I don't know what I expected a Greenwich Village church catering to disparate immigrant populations to look like, but it wasn't this. This structure was more than awe-inspiring. It was imposing. Commanding. Intimidating, even.

Get on with it, I told myself. Waffling around on the sidewalk wasn't going to magically make the church shrink down to a more welcoming size.

Here we go.

I ran up the steps two at a time but paused in front of the door. I turned back to the street and gave Officer Yee a little wave then inhaled deeply. I took one last look skyward, leaning my head back to take in the massive double columns that flanked the door and the tall, stained-glass windows, then I pushed on the door and entered the dim narthex.

As soon as the door closed behind me, that uniquely churchy quiet filled my ears. I hesitated for a moment, wondering where everyone was. Officer Jennings came clattering down the stairs from the clerestory—you know, the loft-type place where the choir stands? I wasn't Catholic, but I did go through an architecture kick before I settled on my major, so I at least knew what the parts of the church were called. But that was about all I knew.

"Thyme, you're early. Good." She strode across the vestibule and clapped me on the shoulder. "Come with me."

She led me toward the nave, pausing to dip her fingers into the receptacle of holy water and make the sign of the cross while I stood there awkwardly. We crossed the threshold and I heard myself gasp.

The main worship space was all marble columns, intricate murals, and detailed frescoes.

"Amazing, right?"

"It's breathtaking."

We stood in shared silence for a moment. Then Officer Thompson appeared beside us.

"Jeez, Jerry. Don't sneak up on me like that," Officer Jennings snapped, her right hand on her gun holster.

"You need to switch to decaf, Jennings." He shook his head at her then smiled at me. "How are you doin', Thyme? Holding up okay?"

"I guess so. Ready for this to be over."

"Gotcha. I got a call from Victor's babysitter. They're stuck in traffic over by the law school. Some kind of student protest."

"Lawyers protesting? Sounds suspicious," I joked.

"Must be feeling left out because the other 99 percent have all the fun," Officer Jennings added.

"Yeah, it's a laugh riot. I told Martinson to use that shiny thing on the top of his car and make some noise. It's an embarrassment. An officer getting stuck in traffic? Shameful."

I took a closer look at Officer Thompson, who had struck me from the get-go as even-keeled and easygoing. A faint red hue stained his dusky skin. He was really angry.

"Are *you* okay?" I asked in a low voice, pulling him away from his partner. I'd spent enough time with the two of them to know that if she participated in the conversation it would be nothing but escalating bravado and back-and-forth insults.

"I'm fine. No, great. I'm great. Ready to rock and roll." He flashed a smile.

"If you're serious about acting, you need to take some lessons, officer. You're obviously distressed about something, and I doubt it's the fact that Victor's stuck in traffic. It's not even ten o'clock yet."

He twisted his mouth into a wry smile. "Busted me, huh? It's no big deal, just some bureaucratic BS."

"You mean the fact that Mr. Mayor has the hots for some actress?"

"Something like that."

"But, the plan is still solid, right? Cate's bringing Audra. We have to make sure she's not in any danger."

"I know." He shook his head and grimaced. "Rich people. No common sense at all, that woman. Yeah, I have two plainclothes officers on the catering team to cover the Whittier-Clays. Only problem is, I had to pull them from outside the unit, too. We had to scramble so they went straight from their precinct to the caterer's place. I haven't personally briefed them. And now I can't find them. I was just headed downstairs to Father Demo Hall to look for them." He jerked his thumb toward a set of stairs that presumably led to the basement.

Jennings came walking over. "You two girls done gossiping? The brother just rolled up. The Whittier-Clays' limo is right behind him."

Thompson checked his watch. "They're early," he said grimly.

"Who comes fashionably late to a fake funeral, Jerry?"

The question hung on the air as the doors opened and the Whittier-Clay family swept into the gathering space with Victor on their heels. Audra's face was pale white, and she clung to her father's hand. Cate gave me a tight smile as she walked right past me. Officer Thompson trotted after her.

"No nanny?" I said to Victor when he stopped beside me. I pretended not to notice when he slipped his arm around my waist.

"Cate sent her to get cheese."

"Pardon?"

"Murray's Cheese Shop is right around the corner. I guess she's out of Gouda or something. I don't know."

I bit my tongue. We had bigger problems than Cate's cheese obsession.

"How'd you sleep?" he asked, nuzzling my neck.

I smiled but pulled away. "We're in a church."

"For a fake funeral vigil, don't forget. We're already in trouble."

"Still. Let's fake being appropriate."

"Are you even Catholic?" he asked.

I snorted. "Not even a little bit."

"You can't be a little bit Catholic," he told me. He pulled me by the hand. "Come on, let's go check out the altar."

"Why? Oh, no. There's not an empty casket up there, is there? There is, isn't there?" I squinted into the shadowy worship area.

"I didn't know they were bringing Audra. The police borrowed it from some zombie movie shooting in Williamsburg," he explained out of the side of his mouth. We skirted the central nave, where the Whittier-Clays were milling about, talking with Officer Thompson and headed up the narrow aisle on the far left side.

"Nice," I mumbled back. "Uh-oh. Where'd you get all those flowers?"

The altar was flanked by four enormous floral arrangements in stone urns. Fragrant lilies, gladioli, and roses spilled out. The closer we drew, the more watery my eyes grew, until we were standing next to the flowers. By then, tears were streaming down my face.

"Thyme?" he asked in a concerned voice.

"Allergies," I wheezed as my throat started to close.

He grabbed my elbow and led me back down the aisle and out onto the church's front steps. I took big, greedy gulps of fresh air. He stood by my side looking worried and frustrated.

"You're allergic to flowers?"

"Not all of them. Wildflowers, surprisingly, don't bother me," I croaked.

"What can I do?"

I shook my head and exhaled as the tightness in my chest loosened. "I'm okay."

He rubbed my back. "Are you sure?"

I nodded and raised my head in time to see Lynn, Helena's actress friend approaching the stairs from the sidewalk. She nodded a greeting in my general direction and pulled Victor into a hug.

"I'm so sorry," she said in a shaky voice. "What ... what happened? The obituary didn't say."

Victor froze and stared at me. If he'd had a blinking neon "HELP ME" sign hanging around his neck, it would have been slightly less obvious than his panicky reaction.

"Lynn, thank you for coming," I rasped. "I wonder if I could bring you inside to say hi to Audra? She's inside, but Ms. Whittier-Clay sent her new nanny to run an errand. I'm sure she'd love to see a familiar face."

Lynn's face clouded for the briefest moment but she wiped away her irritation and put on a neutral expression. "Of course. Poor kiddo. But I need to tell Victor something first." She looked at me sharply as if she were making some sort of judgment. "Actually, I guess you should both hear this—seeing as how you're his sidekick and all."

I wasn't about to exert my strained throat to respond to that, so I just looked at her. She turned back to Victor.

"There's something I should have told you on Monday night, but I promised Helena I wouldn't."

He blinked. "What is it?"

"Okay. What I told you was true, for the most part. We did get mani/pedis. She was acting weird. She did get a voicemail that upset her."

We waited for a moment to see if she would go on, but she bit her lower lip and shifted her gaze to the ground.

"But?" I prompted gently.

"But I didn't tell you everything. The call came before she decided we had to go to Target. We were walking to this Thai restaurant we both like and she pulled up her voicemail and listened to it. Then she just started freaking out. She told me she used to be married to a really bad guy. Is that true?"

Victor swallowed and nodded but didn't speak.

"She said she moved here to get away from him but that he'd found her. The message was from him. She didn't tell me exactly what he said, but I could tell he'd threatened her. She was all shaky and panicky. She made me promise not to tell you."

"Why?" he croaked. "I could have helped her."

Lynn shook her head. "No. She was adamant that she didn't want to involve you. She said her ex would kill you if he knew you helped her. Did he ... is that what happened to her?"

Victor rubbed his palm across his eyes.

"Lynn, it's kind of important. What else did she tell you?" I tried to draw her attention back to her story.

"Um, she said she had to disappear before he got to her. She didn't know what to do. And then I had an idea."

I stared at her. Of course. She was an actress.

"You made the stage blood," I said.

"Right. We went to Target and got the blender and a bedding set from the clearance section. The plan was to stage a scene at her place that made it look like she'd been attacked and then hightail it out of town."

"Why, exactly?" I asked.

"We thought if he came to her apartment and saw that she was gone, he'd come after her. But if it looked like she'd been hurt, well, he wouldn't want to implicate himself. I mean, right? He'd go back into whatever hole he crawled out of in the first place. It was worth a shot."

"I suppose." I decided not to mention that, as a law enforcement officer, Gabriel Vasquez ought to be able to tell the difference between real blood and a ketchup/chocolate concoction.

"What was the fishing line for?" Victor asked out of nowhere.

"Oh, she had this idea that she'd put the line across her doorway or something and would be able to tell if someone had come into her place while she was gone. I told her that only worked in dumb movies, but she insisted it couldn't hurt."

"So what happened?"

"We went back to her place. He'd already been there. He left an empty ring box by her bedside table. She was so scared that he'd come back. I asked if her if she had somewhere to stay. She shut herself into her bathroom and made a phone call. After a few minutes, she came back out and said she was all set. I told her to leave right away. I stayed behind and made the blender blood, set the scene in her bedroom, then cleaned up. I was in the bedroom just admiring my work, when I heard someone out in the hallway. I figured it was Helena, that she'd forgotten something. But then I heard loud, male voices, two of them and—"

"And you climbed out the window and went down the fire escape," I finished for her.

She nodded, wide-eyed.

Lynn might be high-maintenance, but she was also a damn good friend.

"And you really don't know where she planned to go?" I said.

"No, I really don't. She said it would be safer for both of us if she didn't tell me. I'm sorry." She trailed off and looked down at her hands.

"Thanks for helping her," Victor said in a dull voice.

"I guess I didn't really help her though, did I?" Lynn sobbed.

He met my eyes over her bowed head. I nodded.

"We should talk," he told her as he ushered her into the church.

I stood on the steps for a moment longer. And then, as the bells in the bell tower above pealed to announce the eleven o'clock hour, a lone cameraman came from across the street and set up in front of the church. I couldn't read the logo on his jacket from where I stood but I imagined he was from a local affiliate, hoping to catch some footage of Cate coming out after the vigil.

Game time.

An inordinately cheerful-looking Asian woman with pink- and blue-streaked hair bounced up the stairs and walked into the building beside me. She paused and genuflected before entering the church proper.

Twenty

I returned to the church but kept my distance from the flowers. While we were outside talking to Lynn, Officers Thompson and Jennings had changed into street clothes. I overheard them introduce themselves to Lynn as Mr. and Mrs. Elverson. Really, they should have called themselves the Bickersons, seeing as how they already acted like an old married couple.

After I chuckled at my own joke, I wondered how much Victor had told Lynn. I'd have simply asked him, but he was deep in conversation with the Asian woman. Their heads were bowed and they huddled behind one of the massive marble columns, partially out of view.

A pair of nuns wearing traditional long black habits and white head coverings came gliding into the room.

"Excuse us," the taller one said. "The brothers mentioned that there's a child here."

"Um, right. Audra's up there with her parents." I pointed to the Whittier-Clays.

"We teach next door at the parish school," she continued. "We work with the preschoolers. If the little girl would be more comfortable, you could take her downstairs to Father Demo Hall. There are some puzzles and books, as well as paper and crayons down there."

"That's very kind of you to let me know," I said. *Especially since her babysitter's at a cheese shop*, I added silently.

"Bless her. She's very young to sit a vigil."

"I'll tell her mother about the playroom." What I wanted to do was pump them for information about what exactly was involved in sitting a vigil. But the longer they stood there, the more aware I became of my dress' plunging neckline. So I flashed them a smile and scurried over to talk to Cate.

It's like the saying, the devil you know is better than the nuns you don't know.

Audra was halfway down the aisle before the words "play area" were fully out of my mouth. Cate narrowed her eyes.

"I'll go with her and watch her until Janie gets back," I hurried to assure her.

Her expression softened. "I'd appreciate that, Thyme."

"My pleasure." It would get me out of the floral danger zone. And I wouldn't be able to stare at Victor and his friend, whoever she was. They were still whispering furiously in their corner.

I took my jealousy, my seasonal allergies, and my cleavage and headed out after Audra.

~ ~ ~ ~ ~ ~ ~ ~ ~ ~

Those two nuns turned out to be closer to angels.

Audra and I were coloring a picture of a space alien whose body was made up of different fruits—a coconut head, an apple torso, banana legs—you get the idea, when all hell broke loose back in the kitchen. She dropped the yellow crayon onto the table and reached for me.

Operating on some instinctive level, I scooped her up and raced behind a stack of folding tables that were propped up against the wall. I lowered myself to my butt, keeping one hand on the back of her head, then crab-walked backward as far as I could go until we were wedged between the tables and the wall. It was cramped and dark, but we were out of sight. I pulled Audra closer and listened hard, trying with no success to discern words from all the shouting and banging coming from the kitchen.

Then the door swung open, and my heart sank. Four men in white catering jackets came through the doorway. Two of them were handcuffed and being pushed forward at gunpoint. Two of them were holding the guns and doing the pushing. Two of the men looked horrifyingly familiar. They were the men from Helena's apartment, the parking lot, and the Chinese restaurant. Gabriel's men. And they were the ones holding the guns.

Judging by the short-cropped hair and enraged, but not terrified, expressions their captives were wearing, I guessed they were the undercover officers who'd been charged with protecting Audra and her parents. My theory was borne out when one of the handcuffed men spat, "You're racking up charges by the minute, pal. You're going to spend the rest of your punk life in jail. You've abducted two law enforcement officers. That's a serious crime."

"Eh, shut up." He jabbed the speaker in the back with his own gun. "I'm not spending the rest of my life in jail. I'm spending it on a beach in Rio."

His compatriot laughed and barked out some response in Portuguese. Then he switched to English as he opened a broom closet not six feet from where we were hiding. "Get in there." They shoved the two undercover officers into the closet and shut the door.

I could only hope that all the noise they were making was drowning out the sound of my pounding heart.

To my ears, it sounded like a jackhammer. Audra pressed her face into my shoulder. *Please don't whimper*, I thought.

She whimpered.

My heart ceased its hammering and skipped for a beat.

Their footsteps stopped. I gently covered her mouth with my hand and tilted her head back until her eyes met mine. I raised a finger to my lips. She nodded. After a lifetime and a half they started walking again—back to the kitchen. Talking in low Portuguese. The only word I recognized was "Gabriel."

The door to the kitchen swung open and they went inside.

"Audra, listen. I'm going to take you outside where you'll be safe. Please be quiet like a mouse until we get out there, okay?"

She nodded her understanding. Her eyes were wide. "What about Mommy and Daddy?"

"They're going to be okay. The police officers upstairs will take care of them."

We inched forward, duck walking until we reached the opening, then I moved her aside and stood. I scanned the vast, empty banquet hall and then lifted her into my arms. I hurried through the room, thankful for my silent, flat shoes.

When we reached the broom closet, I hesitated. I needed to get her out. Now. But half of the cavalry was trapped inside.

Crappity, crap, crap, crap, crap.

I yanked open the door and did the finger to my lips thing again. The two officers raised their handcuffed wrists as high as they could. I assumed they were planning to pummel their attackers, but when they saw a woman holding a child, they froze.

"I'm getting her out of here. Those guys said something about Gabriel. You have to get upstairs and warn Thompson and Jennings."

They didn't know me from Eve, but I think we all knew there was no time for small talk.

"Johnson here knows a little bit of Portuguese. This Gabriel guy is loitering outside with the media folks, waiting for his chance to come in. Sounds like he wants to see the, uh, casket with his own eyes," one of the officers said as they sidled past me.

"There's a door out to a shared courtyard at the end of this hall. Far left," the other added.

"Shared? Like with the school?"

"Right. Take her over there. The sisters will keep her safe."

"I'll be right back," I told them.

"Ma'am, do not come back. Go across the street to Demo Square. There should be one or two uniforms stationed there."

They ran past us in a crouch and headed for the stairs to the narthex.

I jogged awkwardly to the end of the hall, Audra's feet bouncing off my thighs with each step. I pushed open the door with my hip and stepped out into a stairwell. I shifted Audra to my left hip and raced up the stairs. At the top, I scanned the playground. It wasn't yet noon, so most of the students were still inside, eating lunch or finishing up their morning work, I imagined. But a group of preschoolers was squatting near a small vegetable garden, inspecting the shoots. The two nuns from earlier were with them.

I ran as fast as I'd ever run. The one who'd done most of the talking in the church saw me coming and took several swift steps to meet me before I reached the rest of the class.

"Is something wrong?" she asked in a low, calm voice.

"Yes." I lowered Audra to the grass and matched the nun's cadence. "There are two armed men next door. The police are there. But you should take the children inside. And, please, can you take Audra with you?"

She held my eyes for a moment then crossed herself. Then she crouched and offered a hand to Audra. "Hello, Audra. I'm Sister Anastasia. Would you like to join our class for snack and song time?"

Audra appraised her. "Do you have graham crackers?" she asked gravely.

Sister Anastasia smiled at her. "I do, indeed."

Audra looked up at me. "I'm going to go have
snack. Will you help my mommy and daddy, Thyme?"

"I will," I promised.

They set off toward the garden and I sprinted out
to the street and raced across Bleeker, hoping that I
didn't get squashed by a New York City driver before I
could find someone in a uniform.

Twenty-One

I flagged down a police officer near the fountain and started to rattle off an explanation. I got as far as "ambushed the undercover officers" when he barked, "Stay here." He pulled out his radio and raced toward the church.

I waited until he was out of sight and then made my way back across the street. I wasn't planning to do anything heroic or stupid, but it did occur to me that Janie would presumably come wandering back, laden with cheese. I didn't want her to walk into a gun battle. I paced back and forth at the corner for a few moments, dying to know what was happening inside the building.

Two black and white police cruisers sped up with their lights on, but no sirens. They screeched to a halt. Officer Yee exited the passenger side of the closer one.

"Ms. Field, status inside?" Her gun was already drawn.

"There were four undercover caterers. Your two guys, and two working for Gabriel Vasquez. The bad guys must have overpowered your guys. They stripped them of their guns and handcuffed them, then stuffed them in a basement closet."

Her partner came around from the other side of the car, followed by two officers from the second vehicle. I went on, "They were speaking Portuguese, but I heard the name Gabriel. I don't know if they're waiting for him or were just talking about him or what."

"Hostage count?" One of the officers from the second car asked.

"Um, there's Victor, Cate Whittier-Clay and her husband, two other women, and Officers Jennings and Thompson inside. I don't know if there are any caretakers or priests or anyone like that in the building."

"What about the kid?" Officer Yee wanted to know.

"I got her out. She's in the school next door visiting a preschool class."

That bit of information earned me an approving look.

"Okay. We'll take it from here. Clear the area, please, Ms. Field. You shouldn't be hanging around out here," she told me.

"Oh, wait. I forgot about Janie."

"Who's Janie?"

"She's the little girl's nanny. Ms. Whittier-Clay sent her to the cheese shop. But she's going to come walking back any minute, with no idea about what's happening in there."

"Cheese shop?" one of the officers muttered, as if he might have misheard me.

"Dude, Murray's is just around the corner. Have you tried their fresh burrata?" Yee's partner answered.

"Enough about the cheese already. You have this Janie's cell number?" Yee asked.

I shook my head no.

"Fergus, Oldman, you two close off the corner. Nobody comes onto to Carmine from Bleeker. Got it?"

Either Fergus or Oldman opened his mouth to argue, but the other one shut him down before he got started. "Yes, ma'am. Come on," the guy said over his shoulder as he turned and walked toward Bleeker.

"Mulgrave, you're with me."

Her partner nodded.

"Now, beat it, Thyme. I mean it." Yee gave me a stern look.

"I'll just go check on Audra," I said as I drifted toward the school building.

Twenty-Two

*A*udra was just fine, the school receptionist assured me. She'd called down to Sister Anastasia's classroom to check and told me Audra was currently playing in the pretend kitchen area with three other children. She didn't tell me to get lost, but she didn't have to. There was yet another police officer posted in front of the school, who eyeballed me hard until I left.

Maybe I should just go home, I thought miserably as I stepped back out onto the sidewalk. *Or call one of my sisters to pass the time. This waiting business was for the birds. Maybe the local news crew would have an update.*

As soon as that thought formed in my mind, a second thought followed on its heels: *Where was that cameraman, anyway? He couldn't have left. He didn't get a shot of Cate.*

My heart jumped in my chest. *Unless what he wanted wasn't a shot of Cate.* I craned my neck and scanned up and down the street. No cameraman in sight. What if Gabriel had decided to pose as a cameraman in order to get close to the church?

Your blood sugar must be low, I told myself. The idea was laughable. I might even have laughed aloud had I not, at that very moment, spotted the cameraman in the white jacket with the logo that I couldn't read, army crawling on his elbows through the courtyard between the school building and the church.

I ran back to into the school. The officer who'd been posted at the door just minutes ago was gone.

"Are you *freaking* kidding me?" I muttered to a statue of the Virgin Mary. Then I froze. *Was that a sin?* "Um, sorry, Mary."

I raced into the office and skidded to a stop in front of the receptionist. "Where's the police officer who was just outside?"

The woman looked at me in confusion. "I don't ... know? Making the rounds? Seems he's been walking around the building every hour or so, checking the locks."

I bolted back outside and raced around to the side of the building in search of the uniformed officer. The alley was empty, except for some fast food wrappers that fluttered on the ground when I ran by and, of course, the ubiquitous rats. I mean, I didn't see any, but I knew they were there.

I eased open the gate and sneaked into the courtyard. I could see the cameraman in the distance, still edging forward on his elbows, slow, marking his slow tedious progress in inches. In just another minute or two—three, at the most—he'd reach the cement path that led to the stairs into the basement. I didn't see the police officer anywhere. I didn't have time for him to show up, anyway.

I raced across the macadam, past the playground, and onto the patch of grass where the garden boxes sat in tidy rows. I grabbed a bright yellow child-sized rake. It was metal but flimsy. I could feel it bending in the breeze as I ran. It wasn't a weapon that gave me a lot of confidence. But it was what I had.

I charged toward the man, waving the rake and shrieking a wordless war cry. I know, I sound ridiculous. I assure you, I looked equally ludicrous. A fact I know because Sister Mary Margaret's seventh-grade media class just happened to film me through their second-floor window. "Crazy Rake Lady" was briefly a YouTube sensation—until I was displaced by a video of a tabby cat riding on golden retriever's back as the dog ran up and down a set of stairs.

As I later saw on the recording, I sprinted toward the man as he neared the edge of the grass and launched myself onto his back, landing with a thud and more or less pancaking him.

"Gabriel Vasquez," I said in a tone that sounded certain even though inside I was thinking, *Please, please be Gabriel Vasquez.*

He strained, twisting his neck to look up at me. But I was on his back with the tines of the rake pressed down into his shoulders, so his range of motion was somewhat limited, to say the least. I could feel the fury rising off him like a wave.

He erupted, shouting a string of Portuguese words, the only one of which I recognized was *'puta'* because it's also a Spanish curse word.

"That's no way to talk. You're at church," I scolded him, trying to sound tough and implacable, instead of how I felt, which was terrified and stupid.

It occurred to me—some may say belatedly—that I was really not a match for an enraged, possibly psychopathic police officer. The realization hit me with full force when he started to buck in an attempt to throw me off. I dropped the rake and grabbed two fistfuls of his hair, hanging on for all I was worth. If he got me off his back, it was all over.

Sister Mary Margaret's class was shouting and pounding on the windows. I just had to hold on another minute or two. We'd caused such a commotion, and the grounds were crawling with police officers. One of them would be here soon.

He went limp, but I'm not *that* stupid. I didn't relax my grip on his hair. He turned again, his features oddly tight and flattened by the fact that I was yanking his scalp back. His eyes were black pinpricks of hate.

"Just tell me," he spat in accented English, "is that whore really dead?"

My stomach turned, but I was saved from answering when a heavy, black lace up shoe crunched down hard on his right hand.

He yelped and writhed. I tightened my grip and looked up to see my savior. Not Officer Thompson. Not Jennings, and not Yee. None of the uniformed officers. A very unimpressed nun looked back at me. She was about seventy years old, short and boxy, with a lined, weathered face. She was pointing a shotgun at Vasquez's head, which was also where my hands were. I let go of his hair and jumped to my feet.

"Who are you?" I couldn't stop the question.

"I'm Mother Superior. I'm the principal at this school. And this behavior is completely unacceptable."

~ ~ ~ ~ ~ ~ ~ ~ ~ ~

After the dust settled, and Gabriel Vasquez and his two thugs had been carted off to Central Booking, I went to fetch Audra from Sister Anastasia's classroom.

She was curled up on a nap map, looking at a picture book with another little girl.

"How is everybody in here?" I asked Sister Anastasia in a low tone.

"Our class members are too short to see out the windows, so we missed the halftime show on the lawn. They know something was going on because we heard the announcements that the doors were locked and everyone was to stay in their fourth period class until further notice, but they don't know any details. We like to shelter the little ones as best we can from man's ugliness to man."

I nodded. "Your Mother Superior is a real pistol."

A small smile formed on her lips and she wiped it away. "She takes her responsibilities very seriously." Then she nodded toward Audra. "Audra's a very kind girl. Her mother should be proud."

Would Cate be proud to hear that her daughter was kind? Could kindness skip a *generation*? I set these unanswerable questions aside to ponder later.

"I'll be sure to tell her parents. Thank you for keeping her safe during all the . . . chaos."

"What else would I have done?" she said simply. "But, unlike our students, she has some idea that something very bad happened in the church. She told me about the men with guns. Her parents should talk to her, see their parish priest or whoever they trust for spiritual guidance and counsel," she suggested.

I nodded.

She walked over to the mat and rubbed Audra's shoulders. "Look who's here."

Audra saw me standing by the door and broke into a grin. She ran toward me, her hair ribbon flying behind her. After a flurry of goodbyes from her new friends and a hug from Sister Anastasia, Audra took my hand, and we walked out of the classroom.

"Mommy and Daddy are okay?"

"Your mommy and daddy are safe and sound inside the church. They can't wait to hear all about your day. And Janie's there's, too. You'll all go home together in the limo."

She beamed. Then her face fell. "You know what I was thinking, Thyme?"

"No, what?"

"I kept thinking about how the other veiled ladies are going to miss Helena."

"Uh-huh," I said, not really listening. My mind was on Victor and what had happened in the church while I was rolling around on the lawn with Captain Creepy.

Audra started to skip. When she saw her parents standing in front of the church with Janie (who was holding a tote bag with a picture of a wheel of brie on the side), she broke out into a run. Cate bent down and opened her arms then scooped her daughter up into a hug. After a long moment, she passed her to her husband, who gave Audra a big squeeze.

I walked up as their driver was ushering them all into the back seat of the limo.

"I don't know how to thank you, Thyme," Cate said.

I shook my head. "You don't need to. The nuns said to tell you Audra's a very kind girl."

In a moment of perfect self-awareness, Cate looked directly at me and said, "She gets that from her father." Then she folded herself into the car and the driver closed the door.

I stood on the sidewalk and watched them drive away. I felt someone walking down the steps from the church and turned to see Victor. He looked to be unharmed. He walked up to me, took me by my upper arms, and peered down into my face.

"Are you okay?"

"I'm fine. I have a few grass stains on my knees and some gross Gabriel germs under my fingernails, but I'm fine."

He laughed and pulled me close to his chest in a tight hug. I listened to his heart beating under my ear until he released me.

"What happened in there?" I asked, jerking my thumb toward the front doors of the church.

He gestured to the wide steps. "Let's cop a squat. It's a long story."

He waited until we were settled on the cool stone steps. Then he reached for my hand. "After you let the police out of the closet, they sneaked upstairs without those caterer dudes hearing them. They got Officer Thompson's attention, and he went out to the hallway to talk to them. He uncuffed them using his key, then the three of them and Officer Jennings ushered us into that little room where the altar servers get ready."

"The sacristy," I supplied.

"Sure, whatever. They told us there were two armed men in the basement and Gabriel was on his way. They didn't have any details on Gabriel because the caterers started speaking in Portuguese after they jumped the undercover guys."

That was consistent with what I'd overheard in the basement. "Okay, so then what? Did they just leave you there?"

"Thompson and Jennings had a hell of a fight because he wanted her to stay with us and she wanted to be where the action was. Finally, Cate threatened to sue the department if they left us alone, so Officer Thompson stayed to babysit."

I could picture that mini-drama as clear as day. It was comforting to see that everyone behaved consistently in a crisis.

"Was it awful?"

He shrugged. "It was mainly boring. The cop you found in the square showed up and Jennings made him sit with us. Then more police poured into the church. Given the numbers, I guess they took down Gabriel's men pretty easily. The two undercovers got to do the honors of cuffing them. They were still pretty pissed. It was all over in a few minutes. Jennings and Thompson came and got me to translate the Miranda warning for the Portuguese guys. They demanded lawyers, so that was that."

"So what took so long?" I felt like I'd been out running around the building for a decent amount of time.

"They wanted to hunker down and wait for Gabriel to show up. Jennings insisted it wasn't safe to let us out of the sacristy until Gabriel was in custody."

"What did you guys do?"

"Well, Mia filled me in on the suicide note, for starters."

I wrinkled my brow. "Mia?"

"That's right, you disappeared before I could introduce you. Mia Kim, Helena's therapist, heard about the vigil on Cate's channel. She came to tell me that Helena didn't kill herself."

"I'm confused."

"Mia wrote the note. While Lynn was mixing up the stage blood, Helena went into the bathroom and called Mia. She told her that Gabriel had found her apartment and she was going to go on the run. She asked Mia to make sure I didn't try to find her. She was terrified that Gabriel would latch on to me if we crossed paths and decide I was a close enough substitute to take his revenge on."

I thought about the gunshots shattering the rear window of the sedan and how we'd cowered under the table in that Hell's Kitchen restaurant.

"Well, she was right about that," I ventured.

His cheek twitched. "She might have been right about his intentions, but she was wrong to try to shut me down. What was she thinking? That I'd just walk away?"

I didn't really have a substantive response to that, so I went with a question. "So she wrote the note to dissuade you?"

"Actually, she said she tried to word it in a way that would at least hint that Helena hadn't written it and that she wasn't actually dead."

"That worked," I pointed out.

"I guess so," he said grudgingly. "I still think Mia should have told me what was going on, but she just kept yammering about doctor-patient confidentiality."

We sat in silence for a minute. Then he went on, "Anyway, Mia explained what happened. Cate was getting antsy even though the police had told her you'd taken Audra over to the school where she'd be safe. Officer Yee's backup radioed that Janie was safe and accounted for. So we were just cooling our heels. I was getting worried about you because the receptionist from the school called over and said you were looking for a police officer."

"And then?"

"And then, the next thing that happened was a very angry nun with a gun showed up dragging Gabriel by his ear."

I laughed. He joined me, and it felt really good to laugh. But after a moment his face clouded and he dropped his eyes to the ground.

"What?"

"We did all this, risked all these people's lives, but we still don't know where Helena is."

My smile faded. "Well, we did make it safe for her to come back. Gabriel's never going to bother her again."

"Sure. If she ever finds out. But wherever she is, she must not be watching the news. The coverage of her own funeral didn't make her pop her head up. And she didn't tell Mia where she was going. I might never see her again." He put his head in his hands.

My heart was heavy in my chest because I knew he was right. I placed my hand on the small of his back and rubbed a gentle circle.

"I'm sorry, Victor."

"She could be anywhere in the country. She could be anywhere in the world." He spoke without lifting his head. His voice was muffled and miserable. It sounded like he was choking back tears.

The nun who'd been with Sister Anastasia when she told me about the children's area in the basement walked by on the path to the school building just then. She slowed her pace and shot us a concerned look.

'He's okay,' I mouthed.

She smiled a bit uncertainly but nodded and continued down the street. I watched the breeze lift her veil, or whatever her head covering was called, as she strode away. It fluttered behind her.

I jumped to my feet and yanked Victor up by his hand. "I know where she is!"

Twenty-Three

"Where are we going?" Victor asked for what had to be the seven hundredth time as he panted, hurrying to keep up with me. "Also, why are we running?"

"Sorry." I slowed my stride. "Something Audra said made me think. Where's the best place to hide?"

"I don't know. Is this a riddle?"

"Come on. It's in plain view—that's the best place to hide. Why would Helena leave the city to avoid being found, when there are eight and a half million people here? She could get lost in a crowd without leaving her neighborhood."

He shook his head. "Too dangerous. Sure, most people are strangers. But someone could recognize her—the girl who does her nails or the guy where she gets her coffee. She'd never risk it."

"It's the smart approach. Once Gabriel's men established she wasn't in the apartment, they assumed she fled. They didn't hang out, canvassing the neighborhood."

"No, they were too busy trying to catch up with us."

A small shudder ran down my spine. "Don't remind me."

Once Gabriel's local talent had been booked and processed, Officer Thompson told us they were well-known to the violent crimes squad. They were wanted for the suspected murder of a Latina teenager, as well as a string of armed robberies. I shivered to think how lucky Victor and I had been to have emerged unscathed from our multiple encounters with the men. And how lucky we'd all been at the church.

"You really think Helena would hang around her neighborhood?"

"No, actually I don't. I think she hung around the Whittier-Clays' neighborhood."

He stopped walking and started laughing. "Listen, Helena *definitely* wouldn't blend in with the titans of industry and millionaires of Carnegie Hill."

"Every day when I go to train Cate, I get off the subway at Ninety-Sixth Street, stop for a chai latte, and then race around the corner to the apartment."

"So?"

He followed me down the stairs to the subway station.

After we'd swiped our cards and were standing on the platform, pressed in against the rest of the early commuter crush, I returned to the subject at hand. "So, every day I pass Audra's favorite playground—it's right near the apartment building. She and Helena used to go there three or four times a week, easy. I'll bet that's the playground where Helena met Lynn."

"Probably. Okay, go on."

"The playground is diagonal from the main entrance to the Islamic Cultural Center. When I went to collect Audra from the nuns, she told me 'the other veiled ladies' would miss Helena. At the time I was still an adrenaline bomb, and it didn't really register. But once I was capable of processing thoughts again, I knew where we should look for your sister."

As comprehension lit in his dark eyes, the train came screeching to a stop at the platform. We fought our way on and claimed a foot of floor space. As my hip brushed his, he leaned over and whispered, "You think she's hiding there?"

"I'll bet anything she probably made a friend or two who would have been happy to lend her a veil. We could have walked right past her and wouldn't have noticed her in a million years."

~ ~ ~ ~ ~ ~ ~ ~ ~ ~

When we ascended the steps to the street, the stairway deposited us directly in front of the playground.

"Is this the playground Helena and Audra came to?" he asked, nodding toward the bright blue and red climbing equipment, teaming with squealing kids.

"Yep." I pointed to orient him as well as myself. "There's the Whittier-Clays' building. And right over there, there's the Islamic Cultural Center." The three locations made a perfect triangle—each point was *maybe* a two-minute walk from the next. I could just feel in my gut that I was right.

He stood motionless and stared at the slide and merry-go-round. I knew he was picturing Helena, her long dark curls flying behind her, as she pushed Audra in dizzying circles. To be honest, I was, too.

He shook his head and turned to me. "Now what?"

"Yeah, um, I'm not sure. Can we just show up unannounced?" I gestured toward the mosque's imposing dome and geometric, glass windows. It was breathtaking, imposing, and more than a little bit intimidating.

"We probably shouldn't. Right?"

I crossed the sidewalk to enter the playground and located a bench that hadn't yet been claimed by any of the nannies and au pairs who dotted the playground in groups of twos and threes, keeping a close eye on their charges while they chatted.

"I have no earthly idea," I told him as we settled ourselves on the chilly bench. "If you thought I seemed out of my element in the church, you should see me in a mosque. Or a synagogue."

"Your parents weren't religious?"

"Um, not exactly." I decided not to mention their brief flirtation with Wicca and the Yule Circle they'd hosted one year on the winter solstice. It hadn't ended well. The details were fuzzy but I seemed to remember a bonfire that had grown out of control and brought every firefighter in town running to the resort with buckets of water.

"I don't know much about Islam, either," he said. "But I'm guessing your dress is, uh ... your cleavage ... never mind." He stammered and averted his eyes from the front of my dress.

"You picked it," I reminded him as I ineffectually tried to pull up the bodice.

He blushed. "You look great. But maybe a little immodest for a visit to a mosque."

I ignored the compliment and checked my watch. "It's after five. Why don't we just hang out where we can see the doors and maybe we'll catch a secretary heading to the subway or something?"

"It's worth a shot." He stood and brushed off his slacks.

I stood and adjusted the neckline of my dress again then started walking catty-corner across the park.

Across the street, three women were saying their goodbyes in front of the center. Two of them headed toward the subway. The third began to walk toward us. I came to a dead stop. Victor ran right into my back.

"What the—?" he trailed off as he followed my line of sight to the tall, slender woman crossing the playground.

She was making a beeline for the two of us. Her sky-blue *niqab* covered her hair and the the lower half of her face. But as she drew closer, there was no mistaking her—it was Helena.

She broke into a jog and then a full run, the fabric of her ankle-length dress and matching veil fluttering behind her like wings. She lowered her veil, threw her arms around Victor's neck, and pressed her face into his shoulder, laughing and crying at the same time.

After a moment, she pulled herself upright and searched his face. "What are you doing here?"

"Looking for you. Thyme thought you might have made a friend at the mosque."

Her dark eyes cut toward me for a moment. "I did. Latifah was kind enough to lend me some clothes, and they've been letting me stay there. What's going on? Why are you here?"

Judging by Victor's weird, squinty expression, he was focusing all his energy on not crying. I cleared my throat. "Gabriel Vasquez was arrested today. It's over, Helena. You're safe now."

Her eyes grew huge. She turned back to her brother, searching his face. "Is it really true? He's in custody?"

He nodded. "He's not getting out. The feds here are interested in him for a whole slew of charges. And from what I understand, Brazil isn't in any hurry to take him back."

Helena buried her face in her hands. Sobs of relief racked her body, shaking her shoulders. Victor held her and rubbed her back while I stood there like an idiot, an uncomfortable witness to a private moment between siblings. I toed the dirt with my shoe.

Helena lifted her head and wiped her eyes. "How did you know to look for me here?"

"It was Thyme's idea."

They both turned toward me.

"We, um, well, we planned a fake funeral for you— to draw Gabriel out into the open. That was my idea, too. Anyway, Cate helped us and—

"Cate? *Cate!*"

"I know, right? Yes, Cate. She's super-pissed at you for taking off, but she agreed to help us because Audra loves you so much," I explained.

"Okay, so Cate helped you convince Gabriel I'm dead. How'd that lead you to me?"

"The Whittier-Clays came to the church. Even though Cate and her husband were in on it, I think they let Audra believe you were dead so she wouldn't blow it. She saw a nun walk by and said that the veiled ladies at the playground would miss you. And it just got me thinking."

She raised her hand to cover her mouth and let out a horrified gasp. "Audra thinks I'm dead?"

"I'm sure she told Audra the truth once Gabriel was in custody. Well, I *imagine* she did." I glanced helplessly at Victor then confessed, "I don't actually know."

"Come on," Helena said, tugging on her brother's hand. "I have to talk to Audra. Now."

I stepped back and held up my hand like a crossing guard stopping traffic. "You guys go on without me. Even after everything that happened, Cate's still irritated with me for cancelling her session because Gabriel's thugs were trying to kill us. I don't want to be anywhere above Seventieth Street when she sees you."

Uncertainty flashed across her face. "Someone tried to kill you?" She turned and inspected her brother. "Are you okay?"

He hurried to reassure her. "I'm fine. We're both fine. Those guys have been arrested, too. I'll get you all caught up."

"You don't think she'll give me back my job?"

"She might. Like I said, Audra adores you, and, for all her tough guy posturing, Cate's pretty much wrapped around that kid's finger. But I'd rather go toe-to-toe with Gabriel than be there when you ask. So, best of luck. I'll catch up with you guys later."

She grabbed me and pulled me into a quick, tight embrace. "I have no idea what you did, but it sounds like I owe you one. So thank you."

I smiled at her. "You're welcome."

She released me.

Victor stepped close to me and took hold of my upper arms. "I want to stay with Helena and talk to her after she's done with the Whittier-Clays, but I'd like to see you again."

"I would hope so. You owe me dinner, remember?"

"Trust me. I wouldn't forget." His eyes burned into mine. I could tell he was about to kiss me, but I could feel his sister watching us. I shifted away from him.

"Great! See you soon!" I chirped and then took off at a jog across the playground.

Twenty-Four

Three days later

I walked through the lobby of my building, unsteady on my feet in the shoes that Victor had bought. I wasn't accustomed to such high, strappy heels. I hoped I wasn't going to wobble all night. My neighbor, Mrs. Katzen, on her way home from her bridge club meeting at the neighborhood senior citizens' center, gave an appreciative wolf whistle.

"You're looking good, Thyme. Got yourself a hot date?" She asked in her thick New York accent.

My face turned beet red. "Something like that, Eleanor."

"You go, girl," she cackled as she shuffled over to the elevator.

I teetered toward the front of the lobby. As I neared the doors, Victor stepped through them, holding a bouquet of wildflowers with a white silk ribbon tied around the stems. He smiled at me.

"These are beautiful," I said as he placed the flowers in my arms. I inhaled their fresh, delicate perfume.

"Do you have any idea how hard it is to find daisies, black-eyes Susans, and sweetpeas in Manhattan?" he said with a half-laugh.

"No," I confessed. "But it can't be any harder than walking in these ... things." I gestured down toward my Loboutin-clad feet.

His gaze traveled down to the shoes. "Well, you look fantastic, but then you look fantastic in yoga pants and running shoes, so it may not be a matter of your footwear."

I grinned at him and handed him the flowers. "Glad to hear you think so. Hold these for a minute." I crouched and unstrapped the shoes, then eased out my protesting feet.

"Uh, I wouldn't recommend walking barefoot through the city. Not even if you're up to date on all your shots."

I shook my head and reached inside my purse for my trusty, split-heel foldable ballet flats. "Ahhh," I nearly purred as I slipped my feet into them.

Even though an elevator car had come and gone, Mrs. Katzen was loitering near the elevator bank, watching us with unabashed interest.

"I'll be right back," I told Victor.

I walked over to Mrs. Katzen, swinging the black heels in one hand. "You wouldn't happen to wear a size eight shoe, would you, Eleanor?"

She eyed the shoes with what can only be described as lust.

"Honey, if you don't want them, I'll find a way to make them fit. Believe you me. Mr. Pomerantz will need someone to restart his pacemaker once he gets a load of me in those shoes."

I pressed them into her hand. "Wear them in good health."

She giggled like a schoolgirl and then nodded her head toward Victor. "And you wear *him* in good health, Thyme."

I didn't even know what that meant, but I felt my face growing hot again. I gave her a weak smile and headed back to Victor, who was watching the entire exchange with an amused expression.

"Ready?"

"I'm ready now. Let's go get some Cuban food," I said, taking back my flowers, and linking my arm through his.

"I'm not taking you to Cuba Libre," he informed me as he pushed open the door to the street.

"You're not? Where are we going?"

He looked down at me and winked. "You'll see."

"That's not fair," I protested. I stopped walking and stood on the sidewalk near the front of the building.

He cocked his head and considered me. I jutted my lip out into a pout for effect.

"Fine. I'll ruin the surprise, but our sisters are going to have my hide—"

"Wait. Did you say *our sisters*?"

He held up his fingers and ticked off names, "Helena, Sage, Rosemary. Then there's Detective Dave, someone named Roman, Lynn, Mia. And the Whittier-Clays, of course."

I shook my head. "You lost me."

"Helena wanted to thank you. *I* wanted to thank you. And somehow the party just kept growing. So Cate Whittier-Clay offered to host a dinner in her penthouse. She had Maura track down your sisters and arranged to fly them in. Last I saw, your oldest sister was in the kitchen, trying to elbow the Whittier-Clays' personal chef away from the stove. Sage and Helena were having a tea party with Audra and her bears, and your sisters' boyfriends were trapped talking to Cate's husband about derivatives."

A laugh bubbled up from my chest. "You're just full of surprises, aren't you?"

He stepped close to me and encircled me with one arm, pressing me gently against the wall of my apartment building. He met my eyes with a smoldering look and whispered in a husky voice. "I hope so. Tonight, we'll celebrate with family and friends. I can wait to have you to myself. We've got nothing but time, Thyme. All the time in the world."

I tipped my head back and raised my chin. My lips found his.

All the time in the world.

ABOUT THE AUTHOR

Melissa F. Miller is a USA TODAY bestselling author and a former commercial litigator. She has practiced in the offices of international law firms in Pittsburgh, PA and Washington, D.C. She and her husband also practiced law together in their two-person firm in South Central Pennsylvania, where they live with their three children, a lazy hound dog, a playful kitten, and three overactive gerbils. Now, Melissa writes crime fiction. Like some of her characters, she drinks entirely too much coffee; unlike any of her characters, she cannot kill you with her bare hands.

ALSO BY MELISSA F. MILLER

The We Sisters Three Mystery Series

Rosemary's Gravy
Sage of Innocence

The Sasha McCandless Series

Irreparable Harm
Inadvertent Disclosure
Irretrievably Broken
Indispensable Party
Lovers and Madmen:
A Sasha McCandless Novella
Improper Influence
A Marriage of True Minds:
A Sasha McCandless Novella
Irrevocable Trust
Irrefutable Evidence
Informed Consent
International Incident

ALSO BY MELISSA F. MILLER (cont.)

The Aroostine Higgins Series

Critical Vulnerability
Chilling Effect